# WHY DID YOU SAY THAT?

## More Adventures With Gracie, Kevin, Katie, and the Adults Who Love Them

### Kathy Ahl

*Kathy Ahl*
*11/5/23*

*This book is dedicated to all the children in foster care who are adopted or return to their birth families to grow up with joy, curiosity, and a deep sense of belonging. May they become happy, healthy, loving, and responsible adults.*

# CONTENTS

Title Page                                                    1

Dedication                                                    3

Introduction                                                  7

Cast of Characters                                            9

Let the Punishment Fit the Crime                             11

Great Minds Think Alike                                      17

Look Before You Leap                                         20

It's Time to Pay the Piper                                   24

With Power Comes Great Responsibility                        26

Many Hands Make Light Work                                   35

Milking It for All It's Worth                                37

It's Water Under the Bridge                                  40

Bite the Bullet                                              47

The Worst Lies are the Ones We Tell Ourselves               50

Kicking the Can Down the Road                               58

Will This Situation Make Me Bitter or Better?              62

Crime Doesn't Pay/Throwing Someone Under the Bus            68

Don't Spill the Beans                                       78

Sitting on the Fence/Don't Quit Your Day Job               81

Honesty is the Best Policy                                  85

Don't Attack the Messenger                                  92

Barking Up the Wrong Tree                                   95

Don't Bite the Hand That Feeds You                          98

Get Down to Brass Tacks ............................ 102

A Word to the Wise is Enough .............. 105

Practice What You Preach ...................... 107

The Straw That Broke the Camel's Back ... 115

Don't Beat Around the Bush .................. 119

Two Wrongs Don't Make a Right ........... 122

Don't Count Your Chickens Before They're Hatched ... 125

Actions Speak Louder Than Words ....... 130

A Rule of Thumb ...................................... 134

Get the Hang of It .................................... 141

The End Doesn't Always Justify the Means ... 151

We've Got Bigger Fish to Fry ................. 155

Caught Between a Rock and a Hard Place ... 158

On the Same Page .................................... 172

Break a Leg .............................................. 177

The Ball is in Your Court ....................... 180

I've Got Your Back ................................... 191

Acknowledgments .................................. 197

# INTRODUCTION

Three years ago, eleven-year-olds Gracie, Kevin, and Katie met Greg and Becky Stewart, who turned out to be the "real deal" parents and "forever family" they were hoping to find. Their adventures and mishaps during their year in foster care with the Stewarts gave the adults who love them a **"run for their money"** all the way to their adoption day! Happily, they've been "the Stewart kids" ever since. (See Book One: *Pitch Your Tent in the Right Backyard.*)

In Book Two, *When Luck isn't Enough*, the kids learn about many things that are needed in life in order to be lucky.

Each story in *this* book contains a figure of speech or expression that might seem strange to a child. Each story also contains a little lesson about being a kid, being a parent, and being a caring adult. Mix two parents and three kids in a home, add a measure of Uncle Bill and Uncle Tim and a dash of Father Mike, and you have an unbeatable recipe for this family's success!

The name under each title gives an idea of who is telling the story.

**To the adults reading this book with their kids**:

The stories in this book attempt to answer the question, "Why Did You Say That?" Adults use many familiar expressions and figures of speech whose meaning is known to them but may puzzle a child. This book could have been 1000 chapters long, but I limited myself to just 36!

Next time you use a figure of speech or often-used expression while talking with a child, check to see if he or she knows the true meaning of what you just said.

# CAST OF CHARACTERS

Since many of you may be first-time readers, the following list of characters may help you know who's who:

**Greg (AKA--also known as)** Dad is a detective who works for the police departments of Rainbow Falls and Riverview. He is able to work at home a lot, so he can be with his kids when they need him. (AKA in trouble!)

**Becky** (AKA--Mom) works as a volunteer at the library in Rainbow Falls and at the family's church. She also has time to be with the kids when they need her.

**Beth and Nate** are the adult children of Greg and Becky. They are married to Ed and Julie and have one child each, Haley and Griffin.

**Gracie, Kevin and Katie** (AKA the munchkins) are the kids adopted by Becky and Greg. Kevin and Katie are twins. Gracie is 4 months older. They were cousins by birth, but now are brother and sisters by adoption.

**Uncle Bill** is the kids' favorite person (after their parents.) He is the guidance counselor at their school and is always available to give them good advice. He has actually known the kids longer than their parents.

**Father Mike Ryan** (AKA Fr. Mike or Mike to the adults who have been friends since childhood) is the pastor of St. Brendan's Catholic Church. He is always available, too, to offer advice from a spiritual point of view.

**Uncle Tim** is the kids' newly-found uncle. He was separated from their moms' early in his life and just found the kids this year. The kids have fallen in love with him, too.

**Tara** is the young twenty-something woman who often spends time "hanging out" with the kids (NEVER babysitting!)

**Pat and Linda** own the Bed and Breakfast Inn in Rainbow Falls. They are gracious and accommodating. whether it be a weekend away for Greg and Becky or a gigantic party of twelve.

**Peter, Jamie, Alex, Tristan, Lyra, Laura, Mary and CeCe** are the kids' good friends.

**Mitch and Maddie Lanoski** are the self-chosen grandparents for the three munchkins.

**Mr. Arnold** is the 6th grade teacher, and **Mrs. Wileman** is the Principal.

**Max, the dog,** makes his debut in the last story in the book.

# LET THE PUNISHMENT FIT THE CRIME

## Greg and Becky

S ummer days are a happy time for our three kids—they have so many opportunities for fun in the sun. One of the biggest treats of the summer is the county fair, which takes place at the fairgrounds between Riverview and Rainbow Falls. We weren't particularly concerned when Gracie came home one afternoon, all excited about the prospect of having a great time at the county fair. That is, until she informed us: "My friends and I want to go to the fair by ourselves. It will be amazing. I can't wait."

"Hold on, kiddo. Who will go along to hang out with you?" Her mom, the practical one in our family, had to ask. We'd learned long ago not to use the word 'babysit', which was met with eye-rolls and long sighs.

"It will just be me, Lyra and Laura. We're old enough to take care of ourselves. The other girls said it was OK with their parents."

That was a statement that needed some checking out. Seldom do the other parents even know of the big plan, let alone approve of it. The county fair could be reached by a half-hour bus ride from Rainbow Falls. And while it would, most likely, be a safe opportunity for fun, Becky and I hadn't talked about whether or not we would let our eleven-year-olds go places with other kids of the same age. They would be away from our town, wandering around the huge fairgrounds, with no adult nearby in case of a problem. So I supported my wife's concern that, unless a responsible adult went along, Gracie would not be allowed to go even if ALL the other parents agreed.

"You still think we're just a bunch of babies, don't you?

When are you going to see that we're old enough to do things by ourselves?"

Having said that, she turned and ran upstairs to her bedroom, slamming the door behind her. Becky and I talked about how difficult it was to know when to hold our kids' hands and when to let them go. We tried to remember what it was like when our married kids, Beth and Nate, were that age. Did we worry about them going places without us keeping an eye on them? We realized it was a problem shared by most people who have kids. We agreed to see if we could come up with a compromise that would satisfy the kids and their parents.

Gracie didn't seem to be showing any signs of coming back down to talk with us, so her mom and I went into the living room to read the newspaper. About 15 minutes later, Becky went upstairs to our bedroom to change out of her shoes and into her slippers. She came back down to the living room and asked me to join her upstairs.When I walked into our bedroom, I saw the open dresser, and Becky's things thrown all over the bed

"Who do you think could have done this? Certainly, it wasn't our Gracie, who's not a baby anymore.

"What should we do about this?" Becky asked me, with a certain amount of bewilderment in her voice.

"Well, not to pass the problem to you, honey, but I think you need to handle this. She's clearly a little more upset with you than with me. All I can do is offer some advice: this was a pretty harmless response to her anger. She didn't break anything or run from the house. And she knew she would be caught. **Let the punishment fit the crime**. You'll figure out what to do."

"Thanks for the vote of confidence." Greg left, and I waited for Gracie to come looking for me. But when I realized I might be stuck in my bedroom forever, I decided to visit her room. As I stood at the closed door, I could hear the sounds of sniffling. Afraid that she was truly miserable over this whole situation, I knocked and said, "Gracie, we need to talk. May I come in?"

"Yes," was her quiet response. That seemed like a good sign to me. She was lying on her bed on her side, with her pillow pushed up under her head. It was clear she'd been crying, but at this point I didn't know if her tears were from being told she couldn't go alone to the fair, regret that she had reacted badly and tossed my things on the bed, or was afraid because she thought she was going to be punished. I sat down on the bed next to her and put my hand on her hip.

"Honey, please sit up so we can talk." Surprisingly, she sat up and wiped the tears off her face. "Why are you crying?" I asked.

She took a deep breath before she answered. "I was so mad at you that I did a bad thing, and now I'm afraid you won't love me anymore."

"Oh, Gracie, your dad and I have told you and the twins more than once that you could never do anything so bad that we would stop loving you. Why did you toss my things on the bed? Were you that upset with me?"

"I'm sorry, Mom. I wasn't planning to do it, but I sat here feeling more and more angry. Suddenly, I just jumped up and went into your room. I found your clothes in a drawer and decided to mess them up. It was mean. I'll bet that even though you're going to keep on loving me, you'll still punish me for what I did."

"You bet correctly. You lost control of your feelings, sweetie. You went into our room without our permission, took items from my drawer and tossed them onto the bed. Your dad said I should **'let the punishment fit the crime,'** so here's the deal: I accept your apology for all this mess. I'll show you how to fold all the stuff you tossed on my bed, and for the next week, it will be your job to fold all the laundry when it comes out of the dryer and to put it into the proper rooms. Understand?"

"Yes. Is there any chance that we'll be able to go to the fair?" I realized she was hoping the issue wasn't totally a "No."

"Let me talk to your dad while you clean up the bed." I went downstairs and found Greg in his office. When he saw me at the door, he invited me to sit down in a comfy chair.

"Did you find out why Gracie acted like she did? Are the two of you OK? What kind of punishment did you come up with?"

"You were right. She did a pretty harmless thing to show her anger. Nothing got broken, no one ran away, and no one got hurt. I told her she would be punished for going into our room without our permission, finding my clothes in a drawer and tossing them onto the bed. She apologized and hoped we would still love her. I assured her we would always love her. She's refolding the items on my bed so that I can put them away later. She also has to fold all the things that come out of the dryer for one week. I think that consequence will **let the punishment fit the crime.'** We're OK now, but you have to know, Greg, she still hopes she and her friends will be able to go to the fair together. What can we do about that? Can we think of some possibilities?"

Greg pointed out, "The fair is only going to be here for the rest of the week. If we're going to come up with a plan, it has to happen today."

You could have heard the wheels spinning inside our heads as we tried to think of some possibilities. Finally, Greg offered a suggestion: "We could go with them and take the twins with us. We wouldn't have to talk to them or let it be obvious that we're watching them."

While it was a suggestion, I knew it would never go over with the girls. "The idea is to get AWAY from their parents, honey, not have their parents trailing them all over the fairgrounds. Besides, if we took the twins, they would want to invite their friends, too. We might end up having to keep track of six or seven kids."

We went back to the spinning wheels. With a shout of joy, I began to wiggle on my chair.

"I know what we can do!" I exclaimed. "We could ask Tara to go with them, but keep her distance. The kids love hanging out with her, and they've mentioned that she always keeps her eyes on them, but gives them the space they want. They'll forget

14

she's even there."

"Oh, Becky, that's a great idea. Why don't you call Tara now, before we suggest this to Gracie, to see if she would have a day she could share with the girls?" I had Tara's name on my cell phone, so I called her and told her of our plan. Would she be able to help us out?

She agreed at once and offered several days she had free this week. She mentioned that she had been thinking of going to the fair with a friend. Would that be OK? Of course, it was fine with us.

Then Greg and I went upstairs to talk to Gracie. She had finished folding my clothes and was sitting on her bed with a book on her lap. It would be a mistake to say she wasn't happy to see us. The look in her eyes said she hadn't lost hope of a "Yes" to her request. We sat down on either side of her and told her we thought we had worked out a possible compromise.

"We didn't think you would be overjoyed to have us come with you to watch you from a distance, so we called Tara and asked her if she and her friend would go with you. We know you love Tara and trust her to give you space, while still being aware of where you are. What do you think of that?" asked her dad.

"Tara? That would be great, Dad. We all know Tara; it would be fine to have her follow us around. Was that your idea, Dad?"

"Yes, it was, honey. Your mom had another idea, but I came up with a far better plan." (Becky rolled her eyes—while I may understand the criminal mind more than she does, she knows more about kids.)

"All we have to do now is find a date that works for all of you. Here's a list of the times Tara is free. I suspect Tara will be willing to drive all of you. We can give you my cell phone for that day. Tara's number is on it. I'm sure she has my number, too," I assured Gracie.

Once the details were made final, the girls were unbelievably excited to be going someplace without their parents (a little too excited, we thought) while still having an adult close by who wouldn't be obviously watching them. We asked the girls to check in with Tara every 30 minutes in case she lost sight of them in the crowd. They readily agreed. When the time came, they were so anxious for Tara to pick them up that they would have worn their winter coats and snow boots, just to please us.

When the twins found out the girls were going to the fair with Tara, they wanted to go along, but we said that wasn't a good idea. "How about asking a friend to go with each of you? We'll keep an eye on you, but you won't even know we're around." Since the kids know Greg has had considerable practice following suspects in his job, they thought we were probably telling the truth.

The county fair was a huge success for both groups of kids. Luckily, the twins' group chose a different day, so the girls couldn't accuse us of spying on them. The kids were a little hyper from all the sugar (who can resist cotton candy?) so they were happy to do quiet activities the day after their outings.

(Gracie, of course, had to fold the laundry.)

# GREAT MINDS THINK ALIKE

## Becky

E very once in a while, our kids seem to be of one mind and one heart. They think and act as if they were one person. Take the issue of church envelopes, for instance. Our church, St. Brendan's, provides weekly envelopes for the adults and for the children to encourage donating to the mission of the church and the upkeep of its facilities. Adults, of course, give more than the kids. Still, many adults and children give nothing to support the parish. We've shown our kids, by our example, that to share what we have with others is a big responsibility. We've told them that they need to take 25% of their weekly allowance (about 50 cents) and put it into their envelope each week. We've watched them place their envelopes into the collection basket and have been very proud of their commitment to St. Brendan's. That is, until this weekend.

I noticed that when the kids dropped their envelopes into the basket, they landed quietly, not sounding the way two quarters would have, given the extra weight. On Monday morning, I went to the parish house to help count the collection with two other volunteers. I was not able to make it the previous two Mondays, so I hadn't caught on to what our three munchkins had been doing. Evidently, and this was told to me by one of the volunteers, for the past two weekends our kids were slipping Monopoly money into the envelopes. They were very generous with $100 bills! This Sunday, they put $500 bills into their envelopes and marked them $500.00. We save the envelopes from week to week and record the amount each family or individual has given the parish. I went back to look at our bookkeeping and saw that our kids had given nothing but fake money for two weeks. Needless to say, I was very upset with them. The fact that all three of them did the exact same thing made me realize that **'Great Minds Think Alike,'** Their minds may have been great, but their sense of responsibility was very small.

That evening, before supper, we sat down with the kids, but before we ate, I reached into my pocket and slowly put a church envelope in front of each of them, with the Monopoly money on top. Because those **'great minds think alike,'** the look on all three of their faces said, "Busted." Greg and I just stared at them, wondering if anyone would break the silence. When they began to squirm on their chairs, I asked, "I went back into our records for only two weeks. How long has this been going on?"

"Only these two times, Mom, honest," volunteered Kevin.

"Why the past two weeks? You were doing pretty well with those envelopes. Why the change?" Dad seemed truly curious, but he's a detective, so we've gotten use to his interrogation style.

Gracie gave us the explanation: "Now that it's summer, and the ice cream truck is coming around, we need that extra money to buy ourselves a cold treat on a hot day." (Actually any day would have been OK because they had that extra money burning a hole in their pocket.)

"Maybe we should ask Fr. Mike to explain to you why it's important to give a little of yourself each week to show your support of the church."

"No, Mom, that's OK. We'll use our envelopes the way we should from now on—promise. Please don't tell Fr. Mike." Katie was practically begging us not to turn them in.

"OK, here's what you need to do. For the next three weeks, you will double your contribution to the church from your weekly allowance. If I find Monopoly money or a blank piece of paper in your envelope, you will donate your entire allowance the next Sunday. Understand?"

"Yes, Mom," they all agreed. "How did you know what we did?"

"Even though your **'great minds think alike,'** not one of you remembered that I volunteer to count the collection for the parish. It's my job to make sure the amount of money taken in matches what the envelopes say."

The next day, I ran into Fr. Mike at the library. I told him about what the kids had gotten away with for two weeks and how horrified they felt when I told them I would tell him about their financial scheme.

"They seem to be more afraid of what you might think of them than about what we would do to them. Guess I know who has all the power around here."

"Actually, I would have been very understanding," Fr. Mike replied. "My brother, sister and I tried the same thing when we were kids. Except we just "forgot" to bring our envelopes to church. One time was OK, two times were questionable, but with the third time, our folks were on to us. We had to spend an hour each week for three weeks helping out at the church doing whatever Fr. Tom, who was the pastor then, wanted done. It would have been less painful to just use our envelopes each week! I guess with 11 year-old kids and their developing brains, **'great minds think alike'**—not wisely—but alike!"

# LOOK BEFORE YOU LEAP

## Becky, Greg and the Munchkins

Our kids always seem to be short on cash. That isn't so bad during the school year and winter, because homework keeps them busy, and there isn't much to do in the cold weather. So it didn't surprise us very much when the kids came to us complaining about not having money for their summer activities. We encouraged them to be creative and figure out a way to make the cash they wanted.

After a few ideas that went nowhere, the three munchkins agreed on a sure way to get paid for doing something they thought would be fun—dog washing. There were quite a few dogs in the area around our house, so they thought finding customers would be easy.

At lunch today, they floated their idea over the table: "Mom, Dad, we figured out what we want to do to make money this summer."

"OK, let's hear your idea," said Dad, cautiously, as he looked at Mom and rolled his eyes. (They've listened to many of our ideas before saying "No" to most of them.) But we continued, confident that our new endeavor would meet with their approval.

"We want to start a dog washing service for our neighbors. There are a lot of dogs in our area, you know." (Greg and I could hear them silently reminding us . . . "even though you won't let US have one!")

Greg and I stopped eating—luckily, it was cold sandwiches —so that we could give them our full attention and not risk chocking on our food from laughing.

"You want to start a doggie laundry? You don't even like to do the dishes."

"But this is different, Mom, we like dogs. It will be lots of fun," Gracie said, hoping to convince us. "We have a big metal tub in the garage that would be perfect for them to sit in while we wash them, and we could use our hose to rinse them off."

"OK, said Dad. "It sounds like you've given this some thought. But you really need to **'Look Before You Leap.'** That means to think about the commitment you need to make. Don't think only of the fun things, but also what things could go wrong or be more difficult than you thought they'd be. Let's finish eating; then we can discuss your plan."

The kids ate very quickly, obviously wanting to get started making money. After the table had been cleared, we got out several pieces of blank paper. We labeled one, WHY IT'S FUN, another one THINGS THAT COULD GO WRONG and the last one PREPARATION: WHAT WE NEED TO DO.

## WHY IT'S A GOOD IDEA

--We love dogs
--We love to play with water
--There are lots of dogs to wash
  --A doggie laundry would keep us outside, not inside reading our comic books*
  -- It would be a great way to meet our neighbors on other streets
  -- We would be home, not chasing around on our bikes*
--Our parents would be around most of the time to supervise us*
  -- If business is good, we could get our friends to help us
--We could also have a lemonade stand for those who are bringing or picking up their dogs.
  (Our parents seemed most interested in the * items)

## WHAT COULD GO WRONG

  -- No neighbors will want their dogs washed
--The dog might run away

--We would have to pay for the soap, towels, and water from our profits
--It might be very tiring to be in the sun too long
--We could get bitten by a dog
--A stubborn dog might be too heavy to lift into the tub
--We might miss our friends and comic books
--Making lemonade costs money. We might drink all the lemonade ourselves if it's hot
--We want to quit because it's too hard or not fun

## PREPARATION: WHAT WE NEED TO DO

--Find tub in garage and clean it up
--Make flyers to pass around the neighborhood
-- Figure out a price per dog that will pay bills and leave us some cash
-- Ask our friends if they want to help
--Set up a table for lemonade and cash box for customers
--Make sure hose is clean and reaches the driveway
--Find five towels at the thrift store
--Buy gentle shampoo and doggie brushes
--Prepare a schedule for each week—ten dogs per week (Don't schedule past the first week in case we don't like to wash dogs)
-- Make an information page for each dog—name, owner, phone number

We never realized how much work went into starting our own doggie laundry. Left to ourselves, we would have set out the tub, hose, towels and lemonade. Then we would have stood at the curb and yelled at people walking or driving by:

"Get Your Dog Washed Here"

would have been our pitch. We had a fairly good first week, good enough to want to add another week. Jamie, Tristan, Cece, and Mary joined us for part of each week. It was fun, but might not have been if Mom and Dad hadn't warned us to **'look before you leap!'**

# IT'S TIME TO PAY THE PIPER

## Becky and Greg

Our kids, like almost every other family with children, love to stay up as late as possible. During the summer we have a very hard time getting them to bed at a reasonable hour. Becky and I plead, warn, and threaten them — all attempts doomed to failure. Tonight they had all kinds of excuses:

DAD: "It's time to get to bed, you have several dogs to wash tomorrow.

"Come on, Dad, we're almost finished with this card game."

MOM: "It's past your bedtime, you need to get going."

"Just a few more minutes to watch TV, Mom, the best part is coming up. It will only be a little while."

DAD: "I'm going to count to five, and I want to see you running up the stairs to your bedrooms. One, two, three . . ."

"We're in bed, but we want to read our books; it will help us fall asleep."

MOM: "Lights out in ten minutes, period. And don't forget your prayers!"

We know our kids all too well. Staying up later than their usual bedtime makes them cranky and slow in the morning. Sure enough, this morning the kids were slow to wake up, even though we got after them to get going. They were crabby, almost falling asleep over their breakfast. We had to remind them several times that they had a schedule to keep this morning as they got ready for their dog-washing service.

"You're lucky the first dog is being delivered, because you have a lot to do outside to get ready. You're obviously tired from staying up late last night. We warned you, but you paid no attention. Now, **'It's Time To Pay The Piper.'** You did what you wanted last night—now, tired as you are—-you have to live up to your responsibility to take care of these dogs, to do a good job, and to do it cheerfully!"

How they got through the day is a mystery to us. They managed to greet each customer with a smile and treat each dog as if s/he was their favorite dog. All customers were happy with the "doggie-wash." They paid the kids generously, often times giving a tip. But we noticed that they were too tired to get excited, even about putting their earnings into their cash box.

Dinner was a quiet affair, with only Greg and I offering the jokes:

Dad: "What might you call waking up in the morning? A: An eye-opening experience." \*\*\*

I laughed, but the kids didn't even seem to hear it. So I tried one:

Mom: "Why did the Oreo get an A on the test? A: She was a smart cookie." \*\*\*

Still, no response. They were in bed by 7:30 p.m., no excuses, no arguments, no pleading. It was so quiet that Greg and I realized what a treat it was to read the paper, talk quietly, and go to bed early ourselves!

\*\*\*funnyeditor.com

# WITH POWER COMES GREAT RESPONSIBILITY

## Gracie, Becky, Greg

"**H**onestly," my wife, Becky, exclaimed, "If I don't get some time for myself with you, I am going to forget what life was like B.K."

"B.K?" I asked her, curiously.

"Yes, B.K.—Before Kids. It seems like forever since we've had any time together alone, just the two of us."

"Is that an invitation?" I teased her. "What would you like to do? Go to a movie, sit in the back row, hold hands and kiss occasionally, like we did when we were 17?"

"That's exactly what I need," Becky declared.

"Well then, let's do it!" *I wanted to support her in her time of need. Actually, the whole idea seemed mighty appealing to me, too.*

Unfortunately, it didn't take us long to realize there were three obstacles to our plan: the munchkins—Gracie, Katie and Kevin. What to do with them? It was a little late to ask our neighbor Mrs.Travis to come over and hang out with them, and Uncle Bill was down with the flu.

"What about Gracie? She's old enough to be trusted with the twins for a few hours. We'll be 15 minutes away. She has a phone and knows both of our numbers."

"Really, Greg? Do you think we can trust her to be responsible? Will the twins try to run all over her? What if we're asking too much of her?"

"I say, 'We'll never know unless we give her a chance.' You do want to go out tonight, right?"

"OK, let's ask her if she wants to accept that responsibility. If she does, we'll have to make sure the twins are on board with a cooperative attitude." Becky seemed cautious, but hopeful.

Before we ate dinner, we approached Gracie and ask her if she would be interested in taking responsibility for the twins and a number of chores that needed to be done after dinner. She seemed surprised that we were willing to give her the opportunity to show us her leadership qualities. We tried to assure her that the twins would give her no trouble—she looked at us as if we were speaking a foreign language, yet she said, "Yes, you can count on me, Mom and Dad!"

*We were already a little worried that the idea of some power over the twins was going to her head.*

During dinner, Becky and I launched a trial balloon to see if the twins would be willing to spend the evening under the watchful eye of their sister. "Your mom and I would like to go to a movie tonight. How would you feel about staying home alone with Gracie in charge?"

"What, why does Gracie get to be the boss? I'm the boy, I'm the one who should be in charge," declared Kevin, indignantly and rather chauvinistically.

"Not all people who have power are males, Kevin. It will be a good experience for you to work with a female in charge," remarked his dad. "Remember, my boss, the Chief of Police, is a woman."

We could see the twins wrestling with the idea of having their sister in charge, but the realization that the three of them would be home alone without their parental units watching over them made the decision to accept the arrangement much easier.

"OK, we promise we'll help Gracie and do what she tells us to do."

"And it goes without saying, Gracie, that you won't demand anything of the twins that you wouldn't be willing to do yourself," her mom reminded her.

"Of course, Mom. I can do it." *She sounded sincere and confident, but both her dad and I were a little skeptical.*

Dinner seemed to fly by, probably because Becky and I were trying to hurry things along so that we could get to the movie theater on time. "What movie do you want to see, honey?" I asked my wife.

"It truly doesn't matter to me. I plan to keep my eyes on you the whole time." Becky laughed as she said that.

*Actually, it didn't matter to me, either, because I planned to be focusing all my attention on her.*

While we were getting ourselves ready to leave the house, Becky took a minute to remind the twins that Gracie was in charge, that we were only a few minutes away if there was an emergency, and to put Gracie's phone on the kitchen counter, not to be disturbed unless we needed to call each other.

"Now, for a few chores tonight. Before you can watch TV, the kitchen and dining room need to be clean, the floor has to be swept, and your homework needs to be finished."

"OK, Dad, you can count on us to get all that done."

(*They sounded too cheery and agreeable. I was suspicious . . .*) As we left, we reminded Gracie that **'With Power Comes Great Responsibility.'**

Since it was such a short distance to the movie theater, we decided to walk. It was late January, but the weather was mild and the stars were beautiful. It's nice to take a stroll with the person you love holding your hand. (We did turn around a few times to see if one, two or three kids were chasing each other around the yard or if there was smoke pouring out of a window.)

We opted to buy the large popcorn and two drinks after we walked into the theater. There weren't very many people in the theater, so we had no problem selecting two seats way at the top row in the middle. "What movie did we pick?" When Becky said that, we both began to laugh. Clearly, we were looking forward to spending several hours alone with each other and not the movie characters.

Meanwhile, back at the house, a mutiny was beginning to form. Gracie wanted to do a good job, but the twins had other ideas. "We need to clean up the dining room and kitchen. Katie and I will get the dishes rinsed and put into the dishwasher. Kevin, you wipe off the table and countertop and sweep the dining room floor."

"You didn't say, 'Please,' objected Kevin, "so we don't have to listen to you." Katie nodded her head in agreement.

"Oh, come on, you know Mom and Dad told us to clean up the dinner dishes," Gracie reminded them, and already found herself needing to call upon the big powers of the house—Mom and Dad. When she realized that was not convincing, she caved and said, "OK, *please*, help me clean up the kitchen."

While they moved very slowly, eventually the dishes were washed and the floor was swept. Now it was time to finish their homework.

"I don't have any homework," Kevin crowed. "I got it done at school." He wanted to watch TV. Soon Katie joined him in the living room.

"I finished my homework, too."

"Well, then let's watch TV." As Gracie walked toward the television to turn it on, she felt a Nerf ball hit the back of her head. Her exasperation turned to anger. "Now cut that out! Put the ball away or I'll do it for you."

Well, that was just the kind of challenge the twins were looking for. They smiled at each other and began to play Keep Away. Gracie tried to get the ball from them, and after about six tries was able to snag the ball. The twins jumped on her and knocked her to the floor in their attempt to retrieve the ball. She managed to hold on to it and fled to her bedroom, where she hid the ball in her closet. When she came down, Kevin and Katie had begun to make popcorn in the microwave. Gracie got out a large bowl and three smaller ones. When the popping stopped, Kevin opened the bag and poured the little white balls into the large bowl. Katie carefully divided the popcorn into the three bowls and they carried them into the living room to watch TV.

"Could we have some soda (pop)? Mom always lets us have soda when we eat popcorn and watch TV," Katie reminded her.

So Gracie opened two cans of soda and divided them into three glasses. She carried the soda into the living room.

Kevin reached the couch first. He sat down, refusing to let anyone get near him to share the couch. So Gracie moved to the recliner—Dad' favorite chair. It was like a throne for the person in power. Katie sat on the rocker.

Things were going well until Katie tossed a piece of popcorn at Kevin to see if he could catch it in his mouth. When one didn't work, she tried two, three, four. Then Kevin tried the same, tossing popcorn pieces to Katie. After a short time, the floor was littered with popcorn.

"You need to clean up this mess," insisted Gracie.

The twins mimicked her, "You need to clean up this mess," while they sat there watching the TV.

By this time, Gracie was afraid Mom and Dad would be home soon. She picked up the three bowls and glasses and went into the kitchen, rinsed the bowls and glasses and placed them in the dish washer. She returned with the sweeper and picked up the popcorn. Then, after all was clean and in order, she turned herself toward the twins . . .

When Greg and I walked into the house after a wonderful three hours just for ourselves, we found the kids sound asleep in front of the television. Gracie was curled up in the recliner and the twins were leaning against each other on the couch.

"Don't they look cute," said Becky. "And the house is so nice and clean. Obviously Gracie did a good job of keeping order around here tonight. Hooray for her!"

Greg woke her up, helped her upstairs to her bed and covered her with a blanket. When he came back downstairs, I was standing at the couch looking down at Kevin and Katie. "I think we may have overestimated the ability of Gracie to keep order, yet underestimated her creativity . . . look."

Greg moved to the couch and bent over the twins. "She HANDCUFFED them together! She took my handcuffs off the counter where I left them and used them on her brother and sister!" The two of us stood there wondering what could have happened to bring on a response usually saved for criminals. "Guess we'll have to wait until tomorrow to figure out this one. Let me get the key."

Once the kids were separated, Greg helped Katie upstairs and then came back for Kevin. I walked into the kitchen and found the empty bag of popcorn in the wastebasket. Other than that smell and two empty cans of pop in the recycling bin, there was no visible evidence that the three munchkins had occupied the same space. Happy that things seemed to go well (no fire, police or ambulance calls), I headed upstairs to the bedroom. Neither Greg nor I wanted to lose the feeling of happiness we had enjoyed that evening, so we spent some time hugging and whispering sweet nothings in each other's ears. Soon we fell asleep more in love than ever.

In the morning, since there was no school, we ate breakfast as a family. No rush, no place to go until later in the day. Just as we were finished eating, Greg asked our kids, "So, how did it go last night? Were there any problems? How about you two, Kevin and Katie, did you have any trouble with the way Gracie treated you?"

"You know, Dad, Gracie never said, 'Please.' She just TOLD us what to do. That was mean and made us feel like we were working for her."

"Did Gracie help with the work she told you to do? Remember that it was your mom and I who first told the three of you what needed to be done after dinner."

"Yes," admitted Katie, reluctantly. "She helped with the chores."

"Gracie, what was your experience of being in charge

of the twins? Were they cooperative?" Mom asked, watching Gracie's face closely.

"They took a long time to get their share of the chores done, but they did what I asked. But then, they started playing with the Nerf ball in the living room. I told them to stop before anything got broken, but they kept the ball away from me while they tossed it all over the room. Finally, I was able to snatch the ball away from them. I ran upstairs and hid the ball in my closet."

Dad asked the twins, "Was she enforcing the rule about no ball playing in the house that your mom and I have repeatedly told all of you?"

"Yes, sir, she was," said Kevin. The twins looked down at the table.

"What went well last night? Anything?" Mom asked hopefully.

"We made popcorn, and Gracie poured each of us a glass of soda. That was nice, I guess," said Katie.

"But then they started tossing popcorn to each other from the couch to the rocker, trying to get the piece of popcorn into each other's mouth. I told them to pick up the pieces of popcorn on the floor, but they just mimicked me, repeating everything I said. So I cleaned up the room myself, rinsed the bowls and glasses and put them in the dish washer." Gracie looked exhausted as she remembered the evening.

"So honey, was it then that you decided to handcuff your brother and sister together on the couch?" Greg said it calmly, trying to keep a straight face. The twins actually looked guilty rather than mistreated.

"Yes, Daddy, I couldn't think of any other way to get them to stop acting crazy."

"**With Power Comes Great Responsibility.'** We may have put too much responsibility on your shoulders. You seemed to have trouble with using the power that we gave you. Your desire to get everything to go well was admirable, creative, even. However, and let me repeat—however—it is never OK to use my handcuffs to control your brother and sister—understand?" I smiled at Gracie to let her know she was not in trouble.

"As for you, Kevin and Katie, you owe Gracie an apology for giving her trouble all night long. You broke a few rules that your dad and I would have never allowed," Becky made her disappointment with the twins' behavior clear.

"I'm sorry, Gracie. I shouldn't have acted so problemy." said Katie.

(I looked at Greg and mouthed, "problemy?")

"Me too, Gracie, I'm sorry I gave you such a hard time," replied Kevin. Speaking for both of them, he added, "We'll do much better next time—promise."

That evening at supper, having had time to consult with Greg's brother—the kids' Uncle Bill, who understands kid behavior more than anyone, Becky started the conversation: "We think we may have come up with a great idea that will prevent a repeat of last night's mutiny. Instead of choosing one of you to be in charge each time we decide to go out for whatever reason, we are going to let each of you be in charge of yourself. That means you have your own power to act however you want. But keep in mind that **'with power comes great responsibility.'** Each of you will be responsible for your own behavior. If you act wisely, we will reward you with an extra $2.00 toward your allowance that week. With time, we will give you more freedom, too.

"However," Greg broke in, "if you get into trouble or break one of *our* rules, you'll face *our* consequences, which may include deducting an amount from your weekly allowance. Each time your mom and I go out at night, we'll make sure you know where we are and when to expect us home. You must stay in the house or yard and cannot have any friends over. We might even let you use your phones to contact your friends. You can watch TV if your chores and homework are finished—and bedtime will be strictly observed. Do you understand what I'm telling you?"

While they weren't happy about having to stay home, friendless, they were OK with being able to call their buddies.

"Yes, Dad, we understand. You'll see, we can take care of ourselves."

Bill assured us that this plan would work—maybe not right away, but pretty quickly. We hoped we were doing the right thing. So we decided to give it a try. As Greg said before, *"We'll never know if we don't give them a chance."*

# MANY HANDS MAKE LIGHT WORK

## Becky

Even though school is out for the summer, there are still a few tasks that need to be done, so that the start of school in less than two months can happen smoothly with no last minute projects to do. One such task is to change or rearrange the books in Gracie, Katie and Kevin's former classroom. Each year more books are added and a few are removed to make room for the new ones. Mrs. Quinn, the kids' fifth grade teacher last year, was on hand to guide the volunteers. Most of the kids had her as their teacher for both fourth and fifth grade, so when she put out an SOS for kids to help her update her classroom's library and the school's main library, our family and other families were happy to help her. There were even kids there who would be in her class in September.

When we got there, Mrs. Quinn had made a list of all the things that had to be done. Some jobs involved lifting heavy boxes and carrying them from the office to her room. Others worked at boxing up books no longer needed. Still others were in the school library, helping the librarian file books on the proper shelves. Mrs. Quinn told the adults what needed to be accomplished. Then, a small group of kids were selected to help each of them. At first the kids groaned when they saw how much work needed to be done on a day they would rather have spent swimming or biking. However, Mrs. Quinn and Ms. Jackson, the school librarian, were so thankful and supportive of all the volunteers that we soon forgot that there were other things we could have been doing.

Of course there were a few slackers. One of them was our

daughter Katie. After a short time, we realized we hadn't seen her for a while. A quick search found her sitting with her best friend Mary, in a quiet corner of the library, reading the books they found while working with Ms. Jackson. As a consequence, we had the two of them help Greg and me set up tables in the cafeteria for the pizza we had ordered. They also had to help fill cups with lemonade, water, and ice tea. Afterwards, they helped clean off the tables and put the trash in its container. They had to stand for a long time—longer than the time they had spent reading!

After lunch, we returned to our tasks feeling full and refreshed. It only took another hour to complete all the items on Mrs. Quinn's list. It was a fun way to offer help to the kids' favorite teacher, meet new families and reconnect with people we know. (Plus we had pizza.)

It was a big job, but we learned that **'Many Hands Make Light Work.'**

# MILKING IT FOR ALL IT'S WORTH

## Mom and Dad

O ur kids are full of energy, just like most of the kids their age. Every day finds them off on some kind of adventure. Most of the time they're safe and come home in one piece. But occasionally one of them will run into the house sporting some kind of injury like road rash, bruised elbows and knees, and cuts. Luckily, we've never had a serious injury. That is, until today. I was home alone and Greg was at the office in Riverview when I heard someone come running in, gasping and shouting something I couldn't understand.

"Hold on, honey, slow down, take a few deep breaths, then explain what's happening."

"Mom, it's Gracie," Katie said. "We were skateboarding and went down a little hill. Gracie was doing fine until she hit a bump in the sidewalk and landed pretty hard on her side. She says her right arm hurts really bad—you've got to come!"

I grabbed a big dishtowel and followed Katie to where Gracie was lying on the ground, moaning. I think she wanted to cry but didn't want anyone to see her tears. I helped her sit up and made a makeshift sling for her right arm. As we walked her home, she held her arm the whole time. We don't have a hospital in Rainbow Falls, but we do have an Urgent Care clinic that can x-ray and set broken bones, if necessary. In our case, it was necessary. Fortunately, the break wasn't serious and would heal with no problem. The nurse gave me some pills in case her pain was severe during the night.

By the time Greg got home, Gracie was sitting comfortably on the couch, with her arm lying across her chest. He kissed her forehead and wanted to know all about her accident. Of course, Katie had to add more details about how the skateboard had stopped dead right by the raised part of the sidewalk and then threw Gracie in the air and onto the lawn of the home they were passing.

"Sounds awful," said her dad. "I'm glad you didn't hurt your head or legs."

"Sweetie, we're having hamburgers for dinner—would you like one?" I asked her.

"Yes, please, and could you put mustard and catsup on it, and maybe a pickle, too? Would you cut it into four pieces so I can handle it better with my left hand, and could I have some pop? Please—I think it would make my arm feel better."

"OK, honey, we'll all have pop (soda) to celebrate that you weren't hurt worse than a broken arm."

"Mom, if I sit at the table, could someone help me get some of the other things on the table? I might need a spoon instead of a fork to eat the cut-up fruit with my free hand."

After dinner, Gracie asked Katie to carry her plate and glass to the kitchen, while she went back to her comfy place on the couch.

"Kevin, do you have a comic book I could read? Would you get it for me? Mom, could I have a glass of water?"

I looked at Greg and rolled my eyes, clearly our recently hurt daughter had a painful experience and decided to **'Milk It For All It's Worth.'** She would play on our sympathy and ask us to wait on her for everything. We decided to give her 12 hours of our sympathy and service. By lunchtime tomorrow, she would be on her own, with only a minimum of help from us. In the morning, I would help her get dressed and let her go back to the couch to watch TV, unless she felt up to doing something else.

By lunchtime, Gracie seemed to be doing much better. Her arm still hurt a little, but she didn't seem to need the sling as she practiced learning to use her left arm and hand smoothly. We tried not to laugh at some of her awkward attempts to feed herself. Greg encouraged her, "keep trying, honey, it will get easier every day."

After lunch she was willing to play a card game with

Kevin and Katie. As Greg and I watched our kids, we agreed that every person in the family should have a day when we could claim some kind of injury or illness, then **'milk it for all it's worth'** for 12 hours.

# IT'S WATER UNDER THE BRIDGE

## Becky and Katie

**M**ost people hope to have a mealtime that is relaxing and enjoyable. Our family hopes to have a rip-roaring time! We tell jokes, we argue, we get into lively discussions—often having a good point to remember. Tonight it was a discussion that kept the kids on the edge of their chairs; it was the hope that they would be able to talk Greg and me into a camping trip for a short vacation.

"Dad said he had a few days off, Mom, we should do something. We haven't had a family trip for quite a while," Gracie reminded us.

"Right," Kevin added. "And besides, Dad, we have a tent, sleeping bags, a cooler and a stove for cooking things we can't fix over the open pit fire."

"Please, Mom and Dad." The only thing Katie could think of was begging. It was very effective.

"OK, OK, let's finish our meal, then your mom and I will talk about it."

That having been said, our meal continued as usual:

Dad: "What country has the most fish?"
A: Finland" ***

Gracie: "Why do pigs tell jokes?
A: They love to ham it up. ***

Katie: "What does bread say when it gets too hot? A: Sure is toasty in here." ***

Mom: "What should you say to your sister if she's crying? A: Are you having a cri-sis?" ***

Kevin: "Why did the tree go to the dentist?
A: To get a root canal." ***

While we were waiting for dessert, Dad and Mom exchanged a few words, then Dad excused himself and went into his office. When he came back, he told us the bad news: all the camping spaces at our nearby recreation area were filled for the days we wanted. But he promised to look into places a little farther away from our house.

The next day he called several private campgrounds to see if he could find one campsite that hadn't been reserved. When he called One with Nature Campground, he found several sites to choose from. He looked at the map and chose a site near the river with fishing spots and trails for hiking. In his opinion, it was the best place—ever. We were excited to hear his description of the campground and began to plan all the things we needed to take. We would get our gear ready Sunday afternoon so we could pack the car before eating supper.

Our meal that night was incredibly loud, with each of our kids yelling to be heard, so that their particular adventure would be granted.

Katie wanted to explore along the river. Kevin and Gracie wanted to go on a long hike. Greg hoped to get in some fishing. Me? I just wanted to relax, although I knew that wouldn't happen because while Greg could keep an eye on Katie, the hikers would need an adult companion. Maybe the roles would change over the four days, as the exploring changed and new adventures were planned.

During the night, Katie woke me up. It took me a while to understand what she was saying: "Mom, Mom, please wake up. I need your help. I have a terrible pain in my side. It really hurts. Please wake up, Mom." She jiggled my arm until I turned a bit to look at her. The look on her face told me something was very wrong.

"What is it, Katie, why are you standing here?"

"You've got to wake up and help me, Mom. I have a bad pain in my side. It's scaring me."

When I heard what she had to say, I jumped out of bed and took her to her room. I sat on her bed while she showed me where the pain was located.

"Right here, Mom, it hurts right here."

She pointed to a spot on her right side. I know Katie is the child least able to deal with pain, so I gave her some pain reliever and told her to go back to bed. I took the same advice.

The next morning, the whole family was up early, almost inhaling, rather than eating, their breakfast. Everyone was excited, everyone but Katie. She hardly ate anything and was slow to respond to questions or comments.

Finally, I asked, 'Katie, is the pain you felt in the night better or worse."

She looked at me and said, "Worse, lots worse."

At hearing that, I called our doctor who told me she thought Katie might be in the beginning stages of appendicitis, an infection or inflammation of the appendix.

When I hung up my phone, I said to Greg, "Honey, I think Katie needs to be seen by a doctor. She has signs of a bad appendix. I better get her to the hospital. I think you, Gracie and Kevin should take your car and keep your plans for your vacation."

"Are you sure, sweetheart, you were looking forward to a few days of relaxing in the great outdoors. Maybe we should all stay home until we know what's happening with Katie."

"No, you should keep your plans. I'll call you as soon as I know anything. If it turns out to be something minor, we can join you later. Please drive carefully and have a good time."

When they left, I helped Katie get dressed, packed a small bag with a few of her things, chose books for both of us to read, and got into the car. As usual, hospitals are very busy places, especially the Emergency Room. We registered her and then had to sit in the waiting room for about 20 minutes. Katie seemed to be getting worse. Her face was showing how bad she felt. She was very quiet. Her forehead was getting much warmer. She looked like she would cry at any moment.

"You're so quiet, Katie, are you scared about what the doctor will do for you? I promise you that everything will be fine."

Soon a nurse came to get us. We were taken to a small room with a bed, a couple chairs, and some medical equipment. While we waited for the doctor to come, the nurse took Katie's temperature, blood pressure and pulse. While her temp was getting higher, all other measurements were good. When the doctor came, he asked Katie where the pain was (I think she was tired of pointing to her right side.) He pushed around on her side and listened to her describe where she felt pain and where she didn't. When he was finished asking her questions, he turned to me and said, "You were right to bring her here. I think her appendix is swollen. We'll do a CT scan to see what's going on in that area. I'll go order the procedure."

When the doctor left, Katie looked at me with fear in her eyes.

"What's he going to do to me, Mom? Will it hurt? Can you come with me?"

"No, honey, I can't come with you, but I can tell you how easy this will be. Someone will take you to a room where there is a big tube. There, you'll lie down on a bed with your feet at the opening of the tube. Then the bed will move into the tube. Your head will stay outside the tube. A voice will tell you when to take a deep breath and hold it. While you are holding your breath, the machine will take pictures of your insides. It's totally painless, and only takes about ten minutes. Look at it as a new adventure you'll have to share with your dad, Gracie and Kevin."

When Katie came back, she looked relieved. "Everyone is so nice here, Mom," she admitted.

When the doctor returned, he asked to speak to me in the hall.

"Katie has an inflamed appendix, just as we thought. It's

serious, and will only get worse if we don't act now. I would like to schedule surgery for her to have her appendix removed. Are you OK with that?"

"Yes, of course, when can that happen?"

"It will take a little time to find a surgeon and an operating room, so it might take a while. We'll get you settled in a regular room soon. She'll return there after the surgery. You can wait there more comfortably than in this small room. Would you like to have me explain the procedure to Katie or do you want to do it?"

"I'll explain it to her. She might feel more comfortable with me. Thank you, Doctor Simmons."

"Katie, the doctor thinks you need to have your appendix out because it is infected and inflamed. That's why it hurts so much. Let's use my phone to look up what an appendix is and how it's removed."

We both snuggled close on the narrow bed as we looked up the word "Appendix". We saw a picture of where the appendix is located and how it's removed. Katie didn't seem too impressed with having to have her appendix removed.

"Trust me, honey, you'll be given medicine to calm you and keep you from feeling any pain. Basically, you'll fall asleep, and when you wake up you'll be in a place called the recovery room until you seem alert and doing OK. Then you'll be brought back to your room. I'll be waiting for you there."

Before long two people came and moved us to a room in the regular hospital area. It was much larger, with a recliner that I could sit in while we waited. I hoped it wouldn't take too long for the surgery because her nervousness was growing as she sat on the bed "Would you like to read your book or watch TV?" She said, "No, thanks" to both of my attempts to keep her mind off her impending doom.

At last the surgical assistants came and took her to the operating room where she was given the meds to make her fall asleep. While she was gone, I called Greg to fill him in on our situation.

"Hi, Greg. Katie is in surgery now to have her appendix removed. The doctor felt it was bad enough that it needed to be take out immediately. Katie was pretty nervous, I think, but she's doing well. She'll probably be out of commission (not able to do much) for a few days. I think we probably won't make it to the campground, but honestly, I'm looking forward to having a few days to spend alone with Katie. We don't get the chance to be with just one child very often. Are you having a good time? Is the place nice? Are there lots of things to do? Are Kevin and Gracie happy there?"

"Yes to all of the above" said Greg. The only thing we need to make it perfect is to have you and Katie here. I miss you already."

"You're such a romantic. I love you—will call you later tonight."

"Love you more," said Greg.

So that was that. Katie came through her surgery with flying colors. She had to take it easy for a few days, but by the time the rest of the family came home, she was feeling like her old self. Everyone had lots of stories to tell about their individual adventures and activities. It was wonderful to have all of us together again. The campers were happy to be able to sleep in their own beds off the ground, and Greg was happy to make his morning coffee without starting a fire or waiting for the camp stove to heat his water!

A few days later, Katie came up to me and said, "I feel sad that I ruined your vacation. You wanted to go camping as much as the rest of us did. Are you mad at me for spoiling everything?"

"Oh, Katie, don't feel bad. I'm not upset with you; none of this was your fault. This was an unfortunate experience for you and me, but it's **'Water Under the Bridge'** now. That means it was something we had no control over—it just happened. It's over and we can't do anything to change it. You can let go of your worrying. I'm grateful you're feeling well again, and you need to know that I was very happy spending time alone with you. Love you, munchkin."

"Thanks, Mom, you're the greatest. Love you, too."


***funnyeditor.com

# BITE THE BULLET

## The Stewarts

"Mom, we'd like to go roller skating this weekend. Would you or Dad take us to the rink in Riverview?" Gracie asked, hopefully.

It was a reasonable request, just not one that fit into either their dad's or my schedule that weekend. Both of us had made plans involving conferences and work projects that couldn't be put off until a later date.

"I'm so sorry, kids, but your dad and I are unavailable this weekend. However, your uncle Bill has offered to be your 'best bud' this weekend while we're so busy. Perhaps you can talk him into taking you to Riverview, but maybe you shouldn't mention roller skating until you've gotten him into a very good mood."

"Thanks for the advice, Mom. When should we ask him?"

The munchkins clearly wanted to pin him down to at least one fun activity this weekend. Uncle Bill prefers watching movies, cleaning out his car, going grocery shopping and playing Monopoly. Once in a while we can get him to go on a long bike ride with all of us. He doesn't really like ice skating in the winter, and I had my doubts as to whether they could get him to agree to indoor roller skating.

"Why don't you ask him right after our Fabulous Friday dinner, just before we have dessert? He'll be in his best mood then, and with your dad and me there, he can't act like a 'chicken' or make lots of excuses."

"That's a great idea, Mom," Katie said.

During the days leading up to Friday, we tried to make plans that would be pleasing to Uncle Bill before we slipped in the roller skating activity. As usual, our Fabulous Friday meal was great, and included the usual jokes:

Kevin: "What do you call a walk across the universe?  A: A star trek" ***

Gracie: "How do you recognize a modern spider? A. It has a website." ***

Katie: "How does a pizza introduce himself? A: Slice to meet you" ***

Dad: "How did the toad die? A: He croaked." ***

And that just left Mom:
"Why was the broom late for school?
A: It overswept." ***

We kids laughed, but Mom could tell we were very nervous. Before dessert we laid out our plan for the weekend. Uncle Bill sat there, at first, looking OK with all the things we had planned, but when we said, "roller skating," he sat back in his chair and said, "Oh no, you aren't going to get me into a pair of those torture shoes. I tried that a long time ago when my balance was better and my bones were stronger! NO! NO! NO!"

"Oh, come on now, Bill, that was a *long* time ago, and you only fell because I ran into you," confessed our dad. "You were moving more slowly and doing just fine, until I bumped you. It may be time to **'Bite the Bullet,'** dear brother. Besides, I'm sure they have a paramedic there to take care of injured people. If you're lucky, it might be our friend Andy Davenport."

"What does **'bite the bullet'** mean, Dad?" When Gracie asked that, the three kids sat up straight in their chairs.

"Well, one explanation is that during a war, before there were medications to dull the pain from a broken bone or a gunshot, the person would be given a bullet to put between his teeth to bite on to help him get through the awful pain of the surgery and not bite his tongue."

"OK, Uncle Bill, it's time for you to **'bite the bullet'** and face your fear of roller skating. We'll take good care of you. It will be fun," said Katie, trying to reassure him.

"Looks like I'm outnumbered," said our uncle, as he put his head in his hands and looked down at his dessert. That seemed to soften him. "Maybe it won't be so bad . . . but we still have to watch a movie—my choice!"

We agreed to his terms and were able to have a very fun time at the roller rink. Uncle Bill was a little hesitant at first, but after a short time he was keeping up with us as we circled the room. He was startled a few times by a skater shooting past him, but he managed to keep going. He wouldn't admit it, but we think he had a lot of fun. We spent the rest of the weekend riding our bikes, cleaning out his car, going to Kevin's baseball game, grocery shopping, eating pizza and ice cream at the Rainbow Falls Ice Cream Emporium and watching his favorite movie—*Field of Dreams*—which we all like. He may be an adult, an "old person", but our uncle Bill is awesome! Next to our parents, we love him the most.

***funnyeditor.com

# THE WORST LIES ARE THE ONES
# WE TELL OURSELVES

## Uncle Bill, Kevin, Tony

"Fight! Fight!" I heard the shouts of the kids on the playground during the lunch recess as I walked to the teacher's lounge. By the time I got outside and found the two boys, they were going head to head, toe to toe and fist to fist; some damage had already been done. One kid had a bruised eye and the other one had a torn shirt. It took me a short time to realize that one of the boys was my nephew Kevin. I didn't recognize the other boy, but he seemed to be about the same age and size as Kevin. With the playground supervisor's help, we pulled the two boys apart, although the anger and struggling continued. It took all of our strength to keep the boys away from each other.

Once Kevin saw that I was the one holding him back, he settled down, although the anger in his eyes told me he was very upset about something big. I told him, "Please go down to my office and wait for me there."

I'm the guidance counselor at the school, and my office is in the basement, although I prefer to call it the lower level. Luckily, he was too exhausted to give me an argument. As he walked away, I turned to the other boy to see how much damage had been done to his shirt. While it would take a few stitches to fix the rip, there were no visible bruises, but he looked confused.

Since I didn't know him very well, I kept him outside while I asked him some questions, not about what had happened, but to find out something about him. "Please tell me something about yourself. For instance, what's your name?"

'My name is Tony, and my family just moved to Rainbow Falls. This is my first month at school."

It would seem that things were not going well for him. He's in Kevin's classroom along with the other two Stewart children. I hadn't met him yet, but I saw his records, which had been transferred here from his last school. There was no indication that he had any problems at his last school. In fact, his teachers thought he was cooperative, smart, and polite. When Tony calmed down, I walked him to my office.

Kevin was waiting in the hallway outside my door. I asked them both to come in and sit down. Luckily, I have two very comfortable chairs in my office that are several feet apart. The two boys glared at each other once as they entered the room. After that they refused to look at each other.

"Kevin, Tony, I think you've met." I smiled, but they were not interested in any humor. Clearly, this trouble had started long before the playground fight. "I'd like to know more about your fight after lunch today. Would you be more comfortable talking with me if only one of you were in here at a time?"

"Only one at a time," said Tony.

"I can save you a lot of time, Uncle Bill—he started it."

"You're his uncle? Oh great, I can see how fair this is going to be!" Tony was getting defensive.

"Kevin, would you go sit in the hallway for a few minutes, please? I'll come get you soon." He gave a big sigh, but he did leave my office.

"Tony," I began, "I'm responsible for making sure that all the students here have the best possible experience that we can provide. I promise you that, even if Kevin is my nephew, I will give both of you my full attention. I want things to go smoothly for you. What do you think happened that led to your fight? Has trouble been brewing for a while?"

"I don't know what his problem is, Mr. Stewart. Ever since I came here, he seems to be angry about everything I do. I think he hates me, but I don't know why."

I needed more information, so I asked, "Can you give me

any examples of what things seem to upset him the most?"

"Well, he wants to be better than I am in everything. If I run faster on the track, if I throw a football farther, if I get a better grade on a test, I feel like I'm doing something wrong that makes him dislike me. I don't think we can be friends."

"Thanks, Tony, you've given me a lot of helpful information. I'll talk to Kevin to see if there's a reason he's been treating you so strangely." I letTony leave and asked Kevin to come in again. He walked in and slumped into a chair. We usually like talking to each other, but right now I knew that he was in a bad mood.

"Kevin, we need to talk, but I don't think it should be now. Go back to your classroom, stay away from Tony and focus on your class work. Maybe I can get an invitation to dinner from your mom." When I said that he gave a small smile. He knows that we share a desire for lots of food. Both my brother and sister-in-law are great cooks.

As expected, I got my invitation to dinner and had a great meal. As usual jokes were a part of our conversation. This time it was the adults who came prepared:

Dad: "What's a snake's strongest subject in
A: Hiss-tory" ***

Mom: "Why didn't the teddy bear eat?
A: He was stuffed." ***

Uncle Bill: (looking directly at Kevin, who loved jokes: "What do you call a snowman's dog?
A: A slush puppy" ***

I kept looking at Kevin, hoping to find a smile, but all I saw was a boy who looked like a small animal trapped in a cage.

After we ate dinner, we cleaned off the table and took the dishes to the sink to rinse them. It was Gracie's turn to load the dishwasher. After she was finished, Uncle Bill asked the three of us to join him at the table with Mom and Dad.

"We need to have an important conversation. None of you are in any trouble, we'd just like to share some experiences we've had that might help you at the beginning of each school year. Sometimes we feel like we have to prove ourselves to everyone in the class. It's kind of like playing King of the Hill—everyone wants to be on top of the hill whether it's in sports, grades, or number of friends. Then some kid thinks he has to try to push that person off the hill so he can be king. Girls are no different from boys. The need to be number one is strong."

"Gracie, what's the beginning of the year like for you?" Mom started the ball rolling.

"Well, until Jake came into our class last year, I was the best speller. Now I think he is, but I don't care too much. He makes me try harder."

Katie said, "My friend Mary loves to read even more than I do. She always has the biggest reading list to turn in every month. I like that she tells me which books she liked or disliked, so I can make good choices about the books I read."

It was Kevin's turn to respond, but he didn't seem to want to talk.

"What about you, Kevin?" Dad asked. "What's it like for you in school this year? Are you enjoying yourself?" *Dad probably wanted to know how I got my black eye.*

I said, "There are some kids who are my very best friends, and we like to hang out with each other the most. But we have to work with others during things like class projects, sports teams, and, sometimes we have to work with another person that Mr. Arnold has picked for us. We might have an assignment to do something with someone who is not one of our good friends." After saying that, he looked down at his hands.

Our parents and Uncle Bill looked at him with concern on their faces.

"What about it, Kevin, is anything going on in your class related to THAT?" asked Mom, and pointed to my eye. "Would you tell us about how you got that very colorful bruise? Were you fighting with someone—and why?"

"I got into a fight with this new guy in my class. His name is Tony. He thinks he knows everything and is the best at everything. He's just a big show-off. We started arguing and that led to a fight. I guess I started it by pushing him away from me. I can't stand him."

"What makes you think he's the best at everything?" asked Dad. "Do you feel as if you have to compete with him to be the best one in the class? Do you want to be the King of the Hill?"

"I guess you're right, Dad. I do feel like I have to try so hard to be better than he is in class, on the playground, on the baseball diamond and the football field. He just seems to know everything. I used to be one of the best athletes, the smartest kid in math and science. I keep telling myself that he's better than I am. Now, I'm not good enough."

"OK, kiddo, let's stop right here," said Uncle Bill. "This is the reason we decided to have this talk with each of you. Too often we lose our confidence in our abilities, and we start to question how good we are at anything. In our heads, where no one else can hear us, we think, *"I'm no good or not good enough...I could never do that...he's so much better...there's no point in trying...I think I should quit."* Soon we may be saying those things out loud so that others can hear us. Storyteller Richard Bach has a n important saying: **'The worst lies are the ones we tell ourselves.'** They are the most damaging. We forget or deny all the good things we can do, and focus on what we think we can't do. Please don't let this happen to you. All three of you are wonderful, smart, and talented kids. If there seems to be someone with more skill than you, try to learn from him or her. They can become your coaches."

"When I was in my first job," Mom said, "I began to think that I wasn't very talented or good enough to do the work. I began to talk myself into a lot of negative thoughts. Luckily, I had a boss who rescued me. She took me under her wing, which means she took care of someone (me) who had less experience. But the best part of our relationship was when she taught me to say, "I'm good enough, I'm smart enough, and doggone it, people like me." (I think she got that from a TV show called Saturday Night Live.) I said that every day for two weeks and began to see that I really could do the job and that I was making friends in my office. Maybe each of you needs something you say each day to help you to see all the good things you can accomplish. What do you think?"

"That's a great idea, Mom, can we make a card for each of us with a positive saying? Do you know any good sayings, Uncle Bill?"

"I'd be happy to look for a few appropriate sayings," said Uncle Bill.

Dad had been quiet for a long time before he spoke again: "I'd like to add another thought to your conversation tonight, **'Don't let the perfect be the enemy of the good.'** That means we should be excited about everything we do, because it's good, maybe even very good. So don't let thinking you have to be perfect ruin your enjoyment of what you're doing now. Do you understand that?"

"I think it means that even if I'm not the best speller in class, I can be happy and enjoy how much I love spelling," said Gracie.

"Right on," said Dad, and offered her a fist bump.

At this point, we were all pretty tired of having such a serious conversation. Uncle Bill headed for home, and Mom let each of us have a small glass of pop while we watched one TV show. Then we headed upstairs to our bedrooms.

Mom and Dad went into the girls' rooms, kissed them on the forehead and said, "Goodnight, love you."

'Love you back," they both said.

When Mom and Dad came into my room, I was lying on my side facing the door. Mom walked up and said, "Goodnight, honey, I love you", and kissed me on the forehead.

"I love you, too, goodnight."

Then my dad bent over and kissed me, too. "Goodnight, kiddo, see you tomorrow. I love you."

As he began to walk away, I rolled onto my back and said, "Dad?" He turned around and walked back to me.

"Are you mad at me? I'm sorry about the fight. I know you don't want me to fight—do you want to yell at me?"

He sat down on the edge of my bed and reached his arm over me to put his hand on my hip. It took him a minute to speak, "No, Kevin, I don't want to yell at you. I think your mom, Uncle Bill, and I realize how hard the first few weeks of school can be. It was hard for us, too. My mom sewed up quite a few shirts and put a lot of ice on my eyes. Do your best, that's all we ask of you. If you're good, but not perfect, be happy—it's OK. We want you to enjoy school every day. Goodnight, son, I love you just as much now as I did this morning, and that will never change." He patted me on my hip, got up, walked away and closed the door behind him.

With the moonlight coming through my window, I thought about what each of us had said tonight. I have to admit that I have a family that's not perfect, but it's very good, and I wouldn't want it to be any other way!

A few days later, Dad suggested that I invite Tony to our house for lunch. I admit I thought it was a bad idea, but I trusted my dad to know what he was doing. Lunch was a bit uncomfortable because none of us knew Tony very well, and he didn't know any of us. While we were eating, Tony said, "I really like the birdhouse in your front yard."

"Really," said Dad, "Kevin made it last summer. It was a neat project."

"Kevin, do you think you could show me how to build a birdhouse? It would look so good in our front yard."

I looked at my dad, wondering what to say.

"That would be a great idea, Kevin. I think we have lots of wood scraps in the garage that should be just right for a birdhouse."

Tony looked at me. I think he was actually excited to have me teach him something Tony seemed happier throughout the rest of our meal.

After lunch, Dad disappeared. Tony and I went out to look at the birdhouse more closely. There was a nest in the house, but the birds were no longer there. Tony and I headed into the garage. I turned on the light and led him to my dad's workbench. I made sure he understood the rule that we couldn't touch any of my dad's tools without his permission. On the bench we saw a rough set of directions, glue, and some wood pieces, enough to make two birdhouses. I could see that Dad had suspected that Tony didn't have much experience with building things. I couldn't wait to teach him.

We looked at the directions to get an idea of how the floor, four walls (one with a hole for the birds to get in) and two boards for the roof all fit together. We decided to make one birdhouse at a time so we could help each other hold the pieces together while we glued them. Tony caught on quickly. "This is so much fun, Kevin. I've never had a friend who taught me how to build anything. I'm having a really good time. Thank you."

"I'm glad you're enjoying yourself. I'm sorry it took a fight to bring us together."

Dad came in and saw that we were almost done building both birdhouses. He offered to give us some of his paint or stain if we wanted to finish the project. Tony wanted to stain one. I knew I would offer to let him have both birdhouses (we have one in the backyard, too), so I stained the other one. They looked terrific.

When Tony left, I had a totally different impression of him. Mom once said, *"Everyone is a learner, not a loser."* She's right. He's a fast learner. I hope to learn from him instead of always trying to beat him at everything. I also have to remember that **'the worst lies are the ones we tell ourselves!'**


***funnyeditor.com

# KICKING THE CAN DOWN THE ROAD

## Becky

If Christmas is the best time of the year, then the kids' yearly health check-up has to be the worst. It's not because they don't like the doctors, who see them to give them a good physical for school, sports, and anything else they suggest to keep them safe. Unfortunately, one of the things that's so necessary every few years is the routine vaccines aimed at keeping them healthy and protecting those around them. Of course, even Greg and I would admit (maybe) that we dread the needles, too.

We needed to schedule appointments to see the doctors. The same two doctors have seen the kids' since we took them into foster care with us two years ago, so a real friendship has been established. However, when I tried to find a time for their appointments, the kids began to make all kinds of excuses for why they couldn't go on the day I suggested:

"Sorry, Mom, I have basketball practice after school that afternoon," said Kevin with a look of relief on his face.

"Gee, I know this is important, but my friends and I have to practice for a play we're putting on next week," said Gracie.

"I could go, but please, I don't want to go without Kevin and Gracie," pleaded Katie.

The next week, there were the same excuses. Even Katie had something else to do. I was getting frustrated, so I said to them:

"OK, we've had enough of '**Kicking the Can Down the Road**.' It's time to find a time when all three of you are free. I'm giving you a calendar. Look for a date that includes all of you for our clinic visit."

"What does it mean to '**kick the can down the road**?'"

asked Katie, "and I'm sure Kevin and Gracie want to know, too."

"It means to keep putting off a serious activity, hoping it will go away or someone else will do it. In our government, it might mean putting off working on an important issue for as long as possible. People find lots of reasons for **'Kicking the Can Down the Road.'** But eventually, they have to face their problems or unpleasant tasks."

I'm very proud of our kids. After doing their best to avoid going to the doctor, they sat together and worked to find a date when all three of them would be free. The doctors' exams were no problem for them. Even our kids' shots turned out to be no big deal.

Once we were home, Greg got into the conversation I had with the kids: "'**Kick the can down the road'**—I remember that from when I was a kid. Instead of going home to work on our homework, one of us would see a can or a stone, and we began to kick it in front of us, usually down the road or sidewalk we were on. After someone kicked the can, and it rolled to a stop, the next person kicked it as far as possible. We kicked the can until it couldn't move anymore because we ran out of road or the can got too banged up. Then, most likely, we had to go home and do our homework or chores."

"I hope you learned something today about the difference between being responsible and getting your work done, or choosing to avoid the work by putting it off," I said. *Only time will tell if they heard me.*

After dinner, the kids volunteered to clean up the dishes and the kitchen. This is a rare treat for us, so Greg and I headed to the living room to read the newspaper. (Yes, we still like to hold a newspaper in our hands.)

Our talk with them didn't seem to have been very successful. It took them forever to do even the simplest tasks. Once in a while they would disappear altogether, but would come back laughing. When they were finished, after taking twice as long as we thought necessary, they came into the living room and, rather than do their homework, they **'kicked the can down the road'** by telling us jokes:

> Katie "Mom, "Who invented the first plane that couldn't take off?
>
> A: The Wrong Brothers" ***
>
> Gracie: "Dad, "What did the ocean say to the beach? A: Nothing, it just waved." ***
>
> "This one's for both of you," Kevin told us.
>
> "Why shouldn't you trust the stairs?
> A: They're always up to something." ***

We laughed at all the appropriate times. Then Greg picked up the paper and said, "GO! Do your homework! *Luckily, you can't kick the can up the stairs!*"

***funnyeditor.com

# WILL THIS SITUATION MAKE
# ME BITTER OR BETTER?

## Becky, Fr. Mike and Katie

As parents, we're well aware that kids approaching the teen years can become moody, sarcastic, and unwilling to talk about what's bothering them. It's a time Greg and I worked through with our two married kids, Beth and Nate. Now they are happy, well-adjusted twenty-somethings, who are parents of little toddlers. Beth calls me weekly to ask why her little one, Griffin, is such a problem child: throwing his food dish to the floor, refusing to eat or drink, crying when he doesn't get his way. Nate's baby, Haley, is a little younger, so the time will come when she may choose the same behaviors.

Lately, Katie has been acting strange. She has always been the quietest of our three kids, more the artist than the athlete, more the dreamer than the realist. She's been showing behaviors we thought we didn't have to expect for a year or so. And the bad behavior seemed to increase as this week went on.

"Honey, would you set the table while I make dinner?" I asked her.

"I don't want to, ask Gracie."

This was the first time she actually refused to do what I had asked. I didn't want to get into an argument with her— partly because I didn't have time. "Is something wrong, Katie? You've been moody and snarly for a few days now. Are you having trouble at school?"

Katie rolled her eyes. "Don't try to analyze me, Mom. You sound like Uncle Bill." Then I heard her say in a very quiet voice, "I wish he was here, now."

Unfortunately, her uncle went to a conference in

Portland, OR and wouldn't be back for five more days. While Katie stood there looking a little lost and alone, there was a knock at the door. Fr. Mike Ryan came walking in and said "Hi" to each of us. Then, he walked up to me and asked, "What's on the menu tonight? Can it be watered down to feed one more mouth? I just don't feel like going home to an empty kitchen—oh, I mean — house."

Then, he leaned over and kissed me on the cheek. Mike, Greg Bill and I have been best friends since early grade school. We grew up here in Rainbow Falls. Now he's the pastor of the church we attend.

"How would you like to earn your supper? Take a look at my daughter over there and see if you can engage her in any type of polite, meaningful conversation. Greg and I haven't had much success all week."

"Luckily, I know the meal will be terrific, so I will try to dazzle Katie with my extensive knowledge of the pre-teenager," he boasted.

Katie was sitting on the couch with her arms folded across her chest. She seemed to be daring me to talk to her. I love a challenge.

"How's school, Katie?"

"I hate school."

"I'm sorry to hear that; do you want to talk about it?"

"No", and she pulled in even more.

"OK, you just sit there, and I'll read a magazine or the newspaper until supper's ready."

I sat there pretending to read, but whenever I glanced over at Katie, she seemed increasingly more angry. I know I have a pretty good relationship with all three of the kids, so I took a chance and suggested, "Katie, let's go into your dad's office and talk about whatever's bothering you so much."

When I said that, her eyes filled with tears, yet she followed me into her dad's office, which is just off the dining room. We sat down on the couch in the room.

"Why do you hate school, Katie?"

"I just do," was her answer.

"I thought everything was going well for you, Gracie and Kevin."

"They don't have Mary for their friend."

"Mary? Isn't she your best friend?"

"I hate her." *(Oh dear, helping Katie was going to be a HUGE challenge! I hoped supper was really good . . .)*

"That's too bad, Katie. You were such good friends. What happened to change that?"

Then she started to cry, and her sobbing filled the room. *(I hoped dessert was going to be really good, too.)*

"Katie, honey, why don't you tell me all about what happened between you and Mary. Maybe we can figure out what to do."

"She said I was her best friend. For two years, she's been *my* best friend. But now a new girl came to our school, and Mary has no time for me. She spends all her time with the new girl. Her name is Karen. I hate her, too."

"You seem to have a lot of hate in your heart. Maybe we need to talk about that. I don't think you really mean it. I think you're just so hurt and you don't know what to do. Tell me about what kinds of things Mary and Karen are doing that hurt your feelings so much."

"I sat with Mary and Karen at lunch the past three days, and they just ignored me. They talked about all kinds of things, but they never included me. I asked a few questions, but they acted like they didn't hear me. The two of them sit outside at recess and never ask me to join them. We were best friends, Fr. Mike; why is she acting like this?"

"Did you ask her why Karen was suddenly her new best friend?"

"NO! I don't think I want to be her friend anymore."

"Katie, you seem so sure about that. I hope you won't give up, on Mary. Give her a chance to explain why Karen became so important to her. Can you tell her that you miss doing things with her and wonder why she acts like she doesn't want to be your friend anymore? Give her a chance to explain. Sometimes when bad things like this happen, it becomes a time for us to choose whether we'll act in a bad way because we feel hurt, or in a positive way because we hope for the best outcome. You need to ask yourself, **'Will This Situation Make Me Bitter or Better?'** I hope you're able to feel good about how you deal with this painful spot you're in."

There was a knock on the door. Greg stuck his head in and announced that supper was ready. Katie dried her eyes and thanked me for talking with her. I wished her good luck with her friend,

Becky had done an admirable job with dinner *and* dessert, and yet the mood seemed a bit off. Katie, of course, was very quiet. Mom and Dad were afraid to say anything to her. Only Gracie and Kevin were unconcerned about the drama taking place in their home. They kept the traditional banter going that led up to their two jokes:

Kevin: "Where do mermaids go to see movies?
A: The dive-in" ***

Gracie: "Why was the daddy caterpillar so upset? A: All his kids needed new shoes." ***

When Katie remained silent, Greg jumped in:
"What is a math teacher's favorite sport?
A: Figure skating" ***

Fr. Mike: "Why is heaven always so tidy?
A: Because cleanliness is next to Godliness" ***

Normally, I would go home soon after eating, but tonight I was still concerned about Katie and her dilemma. "Katie, why don't you and I continue our earlier discussion?"

Whether she was happy about that or not, I couldn't tell. But she followed me back into her dad's office.

"I think you should take control of this situation and call your friend Mary. Tell her what you told me about not understanding why she suddenly likes spending time with Karen and seems to have turned her back on you. What do you think?"

"I think that would be very scary, Fr. Mike. I don't think I can do it yet."

"It does take courage. Be brave, Katie—call her."

As she phoned Mary, I could see she was very nervous. I really had no idea of what she might actually say. Amazingly, Katie never had a chance to say more than "Hi, Mary, it's Katie," when Mary began to take over the whole conversation: "Oh, Katie, I'm so glad you called. I know I haven't done much with you lately, but I have some great news. You know Karen, that new girl at school? She's my cousin! Her family just moved to Rainbow Falls for six months while her dad works at the Research Park. Her mom is a nurse, so she hopes to work at the Urgent Care Center here in town. I haven't seen Karen in three years because they live so far away. We were eight the last time we were together, so we've had a lot of catching up to do. She has a dog and a cat, and, oh, yeah, three brothers. I want you to meet her. I hope you'll like her."

The look on Katie's face changed from scared to relieved to joyful. She smiled broadly and said, "That's a great idea, Mary, I can't wait to meet your cousin. The three of us will have lots of fun together. See you tomorrow."

As Katie hung up the phone, she turned to me and repeated everything Mary had said. "Karen is her cousin! Mary still wants to be my friend! Thank you for suggesting I should call her. I feel so much better."

"I'm proud of you, honey, you did the hard thing because you knew it was the right thing. Well done, munchkin."

Finally, I said goodbye to everyone and left for home, feeling confident that I had earned my meal.

\*\*\*funnyeditor.com

# CRIME DOESN'T PAY/THROWING
# SOMEONE UNDER THE BUS

## Kevin and Greg

E ven though some people might think that summer is the best time to be outside with your friends, I think anytime is a great time to have fun. Like today, for instance, I was with my buddies Peter, Jamie, Tristan, and Alex. We had a three-day weekend and were roaming the streets of downtown Rainbow Falls in the middle of September. I suppose my dad would say we were "looking for trouble." To tell the truth, we just wanted to spend some time with each other. We decided to play our favorite game of *"I Dare You"* to see if we could come up with a dare that someone would refuse to do.

First, we picked on Tristan. He's the oldest and the tallest, so we dared him to climb up on one of the cement lions outside the public library. There's sign that says, "Keep off the Lions" and another one that says, "Keep Off the Grass. There's a black wrought-iron fence around the library and its grassy lawn. To climb onto a lion required strength, agility and courage. Tristan had all of those. Alex offered to stand guard at the library door in case the librarian, Thelma Ann, might walk past the door and see Tristan performing his stunt. It only took him a minute to climb onto the lion's back and sit on it like a bronco rider. He waved one arm around over his head a few times before he heard Alex yell,

"Get down, Tristan, she's coming!"

There was a small ledge around the base of each lion. Tristan slid down the side opposite the steps and clung by his fingertips to the lion's mane. When Alex gave him the all clear sign and hurried down the steps, Tristan jumped to the grass and sprinted to the fence. We were able to help him get over the spikey tips of the fence. Then we stood there patting him on the back and congratulating him,

"Good job, good job!"

Next, we challenged Peter to go into the old Albers' house, which has a reputation of being haunted. "You need to find a way into the house, and bring back the toilet paper roller (spindle) in the upstairs bathroom."

(We assumed there was a bathroom upstairs and figured no one would have thought to remove the roller from the holder when the Albers family moved out.) It would be proof that he had gotten into the house and made it to the second floor. As with the library, there was a fence around the property, but this was a white picket fence with a gate. As we stood there daring him with our eyes, he opened the gate and climbed the steps to the front door. It was locked. The windows on the front of the house were boarded up, so he began to explore the huge wraparound porch. On the right side, he found a window where the board had loosened enough that he was able to wiggle through into the living room. He looked around as if expecting to see ghosts welcoming him into their home. Seeing nothing unusual, Peter hurried up to the second floor, found the bathroom and the treasured toilet paper roller in its holder. He grabbed it and ran downstairs to the same window and crawled out. In a flash, he was back on the sidewalk,

"I did it! I did it! See!" He stood there waving around the proof of his success. As we did with Tristan, we stood around Peter congratulating him and patting him on the back.

When there were three of us left to face a challenge, Tristan and Peter put their heads together and came up with the ultimate dare: "We dare you, Jamie, Alex and Kevin to go into Mr. Johnson's grocery store and sneak out with three candy bars."

This was a dare that could have serious consequences, more serious than the first two, although if Tristan had been caught by the librarian or Peter met by a group of ghosts, then maybe our dare wasn't all that bad. The three of us walked into the store, looked at a few comic books, then passed along the candy shelves. When we thought no one was looking, each of us grabbed a candy bar and slipped it into a pocket. Then, trying to keep from looking guilty or in a hurry, we walked out the front door onto the sidewalk. When, we looked down the street, we saw Peter and Tristan at the corner waiting for us. We hurried away from the store, expecting an angry Mr. Johnson to run after us yelling, "Stop!" But that's not what happened— no one paid any attention to us as we ran around the corner, crossed the street and headed for the alley behind the Ice Cream Emporium. Our hearts were pounding with fear and relief at having completed our dare.

"We did it, but it was so scary. I kept thinking someone would shout at us and start yelling: 'Police, Police!'" Alex spoke with a very shaky voice.

Jamie, Alex and I brought out our candy bars. Our plan was to share each bar with someone else. However, there was a problem—there were only five of us. I had no one who could share my other half. It was then that I saw Katie walking toward us. She was on the way to the store to get a loaf of bread for Mom and saw us leaving the store in a hurry. She followed us to the alley and immediately figured out what the five of us were doing. Since I had a half of a candy bar in my hand, I offered it to her:

"I'll give you half of my candy bar if you promise not to tell our parents what I just did." She promised not to tell and gladly accepted the candy I handed her. After eating the candy and wiping the chocolate off our mouths, we split up and headed home.

When Katie and I got home, we went to our bedrooms to calm down and get ready for supper. Luckily, Katie had remembered to buy the loaf of bread, so Mom didn't question anything. When she called us down to eat, we were surprised to see that our uncle Bill had been invited to join us. Katie and I felt a little nervous with him at the table because he's very good at sensing when we kids are acting uncomfortable. Maybe it was guilt, but neither Katie nor I could look at the adults as we ate. However, the supper conversation was normal for the adults, and no one asked what we had been doing that day.

As soon as dessert was over, Gracie announced that she had a special report to write by Monday, so she hurried upstairs to work on it. Katie and I were also about to say that we had homework, when Uncle Bill said,

"Oh, come on, you have all weekend to do your homework. How about joining me downstairs for a quick game of ping pong? I can take on the two of you at one time!"

That sent up red flags for both of us, but we couldn't refuse, since our parents know how much we love Uncle Bill. So we followed him downstairs and began a typical game of ping pong, with him on one side of the table and Katie and me on the other side. He's an amazing player; we had a hard time returning his serves.

After what seemed like forever to us—and a winning game for him—he placed his paddle on the table and said, "So, do you want to tell me what was going on inside the grocery store this afternoon?"

"What do you mean?" I asked. Katie began to panic.

"You know what I mean. I was in the store when I saw you, Jamie and Alex take three candy bars out of the store. I'll ask again: Do you want to tell me what was going on?"

Since he knows us so well, he knew we would be more likely to talk to him about what we did than to tell our parents. He never yells at us or says, "What were you thinking?" He leaves that for Mom and Dad to say. Because of the gentleness and patience he showed, we began to talk and tell him all that had happened that afternoon including the part when Katie got involved. He listened without interrupting us, and then sat there for a short time before he spoke:

"You know you have to tell your folks about this, don't

you? I think you broke a few rules that they have to know about. Do you want me to stay and help you with this?"

"They're going to be really mad at us, aren't they? Do you think they'll hate us?"

"I think it's fair to think some of what you did will disappoint them, and, yes, they may be angry. But, remember how often they've said how much they love you. They're also strong believers in forgiveness and fair consequences."

So that's how we ended up sitting on the couch in the living room, with our parents on the footstool facing us. Since Uncle Bill was still hanging around, it was a clue to them that whatever we were about to tell them wasn't going to be pleasant to hear.

They listened patiently as I told them about Tristan and the lion, and Peter and the toilet paper roller, but they leaned forward to give us their full attention when I told them about stealing a candy bar at the grocery store and giving half of it to Katie.

"I didn't have anything to do with stealing the candy, Dad. It was all Kevin's idea." Katie couldn't wait to share that information with our parents.

"Thank you, Katie, that's called **'throwing your brother under the bus,'**—in other words: 'tattling.' We'll get to you later," said Dad.

Mom asked, "Do you think Mr. Johnson is aware of what you did?"

"I don't think so, Mom. No one chased us or told us to come back. But Uncle Bill was in the store and saw what we did."

"Would we be having this conversation if no one had seen you take the candy?" She was concerned about our poor judgment.

"I think we would have told you in a few days because we'd feel guilty for what we did. I knew it was wrong, but I decided to do it anyways. I didn't want the other guys to think I was a chicken."

Dad asked, "Are you planning to play with your friends tomorrow?" When I said, "Yes," he asked me to bring all four of them to our house in the morning. All I could do is nod my head. I had a feeling tomorrow would not be as exciting as today.

Saturday morning, the six of us (Katie included) were sitting at our dining room table with Mom, Dad and Uncle Bill. They were surprisingly calm and welcoming to my friends. After a few minutes of polite chatter, Dad looked at us and said, "Tristan, why don't you tell us about your challenge yesterday."

Tristan looked at us and wondered how much he should say. "I was supposed to climb up onto one of the lions in front of the library and pretend to be a rodeo bronco rider. Alex kept guard at the front door in case Miss Thelma came toward the window."

"Alex, will you tell us what you did," asked Dad.

"I stood by the front door and when I saw her coming, I shouted to Tristan to get down. I saw him slide off the lion and disappear."

"Where did you go, Tristan?" Mom seemed curious.

"I slid off the lion on the side away from the steps and hung onto the mane of the lion while I crouched on a little ledge that makes the base the lion sits on. When Miss Thelma was gone, I jumped down and ran across the grass to where the guys were standing. They helped me climb over the fence."

"Peter," my dad switched to talk to him. "What did you do for your dare?"

"I went up to the porch on the old Albers' house and found a loose board that I moved so I could get inside the house. It was dark and dirty, so I ran upstairs, grabbed the toilet paper roller out of its holder, and ran back out to where the guys were standing."

"Was there a fence at the Albers' house?" Mom was beginning to like asking questions.

"Yes, Mrs. Stewart. I was able to go through the gate in front of the house."

At this point, our dad leaned back and seemed lost in thought. We waited in silence, afraid he was going to say, "WHAT WERE YOU THINKING?" Instead, he smiled and said, "Well, these two dares were harmless enough, although, you could be arrested for trespassing on city AND private property. There are pretty clear signs saying NO TRESPASSING in front of the Albers' property and STAY OFF THE LIONS in front of the library. I could get you for the STAY OFF THE GRASS sign, too. But these are small charges compared to the story we're really interested to hear. Jamie, why don't you tell us about what you, Kevin, and Alex were dared to do." He leaned forward to listen to Jamie.

"We were supposed to go into the grocery store, pretend to be interested in the comic books, and then sneak three candy bars out of the store. We would share them with the others."

"Katie, you were supposed to be going to the store for me. I'm wondering how you got involved in this. Please tell us." (Mom was beginning to sound like Dad.)

"I was going to the store, Mom, really I was. I saw Kevin, Alex and Jamie come out of the store and hurry around the corner to the alley. I just wanted to know what they were doing. When I saw the candy bars, I figured out what happened. That's when Kevin offered to give me half of his candy bar if I promised not to tell you what he'd done."

Dad tipped his chair back again and studied us closely. Mom looked shocked. We were beginning to squirm. Finally Dad said, "There's a lot going on here. Let me explain this for you: First of all, this was a terrible dare, Peter and Tristan. You asked your friends to do something that was illegal. They broke the law. Even though the two of you weren't in the store, just being part of the planning makes you accomplices with the other three.

#2. You didn't sneak the candy bars from the store, you STOLE them. The candy is Mr. Johnson's property until someone buys it.

#3. Kevin, when you offered Katie half of your candy for her promise to keep this whole thing a secret, that's called BRIBERY or a QUID PRO QUO, which means 'I'll do something for you, if you'll do something for me.' Both those actions are troubling."

#4. And, Katie, even though you weren't an *accomplice* to all of this, you became an *accessory after the fact* when you ate the stolen candy. That means that you are a part of the crime even though you didn't help to plan it or carry out the plan."

Mom shook her head and asked: "I need to know if the five of you knew that this dare was a terrible idea, an illegal one?"

"We were playing, Mom, we didn't think about anything else."

Then Dad looked at Katie and asked her, "Did you think it was a bad idea for Kevin to ask you to keep quiet?" She nodded her head. "Did all six of you share the candy knowing that what you'd done was WRONG?"

Even though Uncle Bill had warned us last night about what our parents would ask, we joined our other friends who looked down at their hands folded in their laps. No one wanted to be the first one to speak. I looked up at Uncle Bill, and he nodded his head to encourage me to talk: "I thought it was wrong, Dad. I knew we were stealing the candy, but I didn't want the others to think that I wasn't brave enough to go into the store." I lowered my head again.

"I guess I knew it was wrong, too, Mr. Stewart, but we had dared Peter and Tristan, so I thought we had to do what they said," admitted Jamie. "I went along with my friends."

Alex looked like he was too afraid to talk, so Mom said quietly, "Is that what happened to you, Alex, did you just go along with your friends?" Alex looked at her and said, "Yes."

Katie was ready to burst into tears because she knew it would be her turn to tell her story.

"OK, Katie, tell us just what YOU did. Try not to tell us what the others did; they already told us their story."

Katie took a deep breath and said, "I was going to the store when I saw some boys coming out of the store. I decided to follow them to see what they were doing. When I caught up with them, they were beginning to split some candy bars. One boy offered me half of his candy. I can't tell you any more because I can't say what that one boy said . . . I ate the candy." My dad looked at my mom and rolled his eyes. Uncle Bill smiled.

Dad sighed and said, "Yesterday's play showed an incredible use of poor judgment. I think all six of you owe Mr. Johnson an apology and $1 each."

"But, Dad, we only took three candy bars. That's $3, not $6."

Kevin might have said it, but the rest of us nodded in agreement.

The three adults looked at us sternly. Finally, Dad spoke, "Like I said before: each of you owes Mr. Johnson $1 from your allowance, plus an apology. I'm going to call your parents, but you four boys need to fill them in and tell them my advice for handling this situation. If they decide to do anything else to punish you, that will be up to them."

My friends nodded their heads and got up to leave. Peter looked at my dad and said, "I'm sorry, Mr. Stewart. I won't do it again." Every one of us added our "I'm sorry" to Peter's.

After my friends left, Uncle Bill took off for home. Mom looked at Katie and me and said, "Since you already had a good time with candy yesterday, I think you should go without any sweets this weekend—including the donut after church on Sunday. Since what you did was seriously wrong, I think the two of you should find a time to talk to Fr. Mike together and let him know what you did. I'm sure he'll give you some good advice."

We went to our rooms and considered ourselves lucky that we didn't get a more severe punishment. Both of us looked at our allowance jars. $1.00 would take a big chunk out of our savings. Kevin came into my room and said, "Katie, I know we enjoyed a little chocolate yesterday, but considering what happened today, especially to our allowance, I think it's fair to say, **'Crime Doesn't Pay!'"**

# DON'T SPILL THE BEANS

## Uncle Bill

G reg and Becky's wedding anniversary is coming up in two weeks. It's getting increasingly hard to think of a gift for them, since they already have all that they need in major areas of their life—household items, electronics, gift cards, three wonderful munchkins, two grown kids, two grandkids—and me.

The only thing I thought they might need is TIME— a time for them to be alone, just the two of them, in a setting that requires no responsibilities, no kids, and no thought of what might be waiting for them when they get home. I would offer to stay with the kids, make sure they do their chores on Saturday, go shopping for meals, make sure the kitchen, living room and bedrooms are kept clean and neat, and eat out at least once. It would be a busy Friday night until Sunday afternoon, but I feel up to the challenge. Trouble is, I made a reservation for the two of them at the Rainbow Falls Bed and Breakfast last week, and now I have to keep my plan a secret, not just from Becky and Greg, but from their five kids, too. I plan to reveal my secret this week at our Fabulous Friday dinner. We have this special meal almost every Friday, usually with a dessert that makes the meal "fabulous."

The younger kids came to me last week and asked me what they could get their parents for their anniversary. Of course, they have very little money—their allowance is spent even before they receive it. I suggested doing their chores without complaining: washing the car, offering to run errands, and showing appreciation for all that their parents do for them. They could each make a card for their mom and dad, think of some way to say, "I love you," and include what they planned to do for them.

On Wednesday of this week, the munchkins were hanging out at my place when I got a phone call from the B and B (Bed and Breakfast) confirming my reservation for their parents' special weekend. Pat and Linda, the owners, enjoy the whole family, but they also understand Greg and Becky's need to get away from everyone. While I was talking to Linda, I assured her that the weekend would be a surprise; I had looked at their calendar and saw nothing scheduled. Unfortunately, when I hung up, the three kids wanted to know what was happening.

"Uncle Bill, why did you tell Linda at the B and B that you had scheduled a weekend for Mom and Dad and were sure they would be there? When is it? Are we invited, too? We love it there."

I was trapped. I could have lied, and maybe I should have, but the kids know right from wrong. (And so do I.) "Yes, I plan to give your parents a weekend at the B and B for their anniversary, and no, you are NOT invited. I need to hear you promise me that you won't **'Spill the Beans'** before Friday night."

"What does **'spill the beans'** mean?"

"It means giving out information before the right time. It used to be that people voted by putting a white bean for 'yes' or a dark bean for 'no' into a bucket. If someone knocked over a bucket and **'spilled the beans,'** the votes were seen before it was time to officially count them. A winner of the voting could be announced too early and not be right."

"We won't say a thing to Mom and Dad—promise," said Gracie, and the twins nodded in agreement.

"I don't notice that any of you have your fingers crossed behind your backs, so I guess I can trust you for two more days."

On Friday night, we gathered together for our Fabulous Friday meal. The kids knew of my plan to announce my gift for their parents' anniversary, so they were a little more wiggly than normal. They kept looking at me and smiling. Still, they managed to have a few jokes to share.

Kevin: "What kind of tea did the American colonists want? A. Libertea." ***

Gracie: "What did the baby light bulb say to the mommy light bulb?"
A: I love you watts and watts!" ***

Katie: "What is the fiercest flower in the garden? A: The tiger lily" ***

We all laughed, but finally, when I knew the suspense was killing the munchkins, I handed Becky and Greg an envelope from the Rainbow Falls Bed and Breakfast.

"Congratulations on many years of wedded bliss," I told them. "It's probably time to get away from all of us!" They tore open the envelope and gave me a broad smile. "What a great gift," Becky exclaimed. Greg started smiling and kept on smiling as each of their five kids (Beth and Nate's families had also been invited to eat with us) handed them their cards and simpler gifts.

"You know, Mom and Dad, you could invite us to come with you. It would be so much fun," said, Gracie. Her parents looked at each other and rolled their eyes to the ceiling—they seem to do that an awful lot lately.

"Thanks for the suggestion, sweetie," said Mom, "but I think we'll just go by ourselves. However, we might entertain the idea of having all of you join us for brunch at the B and B on Sunday. But you need to go home right afterwards, since we will still have a few hours left for alone time!" And Dad added, "Thank you, Bill, for this terrific gift. We will certainly enjoy it." (Smiles all around . . .and a special wink from Uncle Bill to the three of us for not **'spilling the beans'**.)

***funnyeditor.com

# SITTING ON THE FENCE/DON'T QUIT YOUR DAY JOB

## Gracie

**"T**ime's running out, Gracie," Mom warned me. "It's time to decide what you want for your birthday. Do you want to have a party or go shopping for some new clothes? I'm offering you the chance to go to two stores of your choice to look for four items you want to add to your clothes collection from last winter. You need to stop **'Sitting on the Fence,'** honey, and choose.

"I think I want to have a party here, if we can fix up the basement and decorate it. We'd need food, drinks, music, different lights, not like the bright ones that are there now— maybe like a string of clear Christmas tree lights. We could even decorate with Halloween stuff, since that's my favorite holiday.

"But, at the same time, I sure would like to go shopping, especially if you let me pick out the clothes I want. I need some new things—I just can't decide . . . "

My mom sighed, "If it will help you to decide, you know that your dad and I will take you and the twins shopping for some winter clothes. However, you will need our approval for those."

"OK, I want to go shopping with you. I want to pick out my own clothes—promise?"

"Yes, I promise. The twins have plans for Saturday, so your dad and I might even take you to lunch at the restaurant of your choice. No fast foods, please."

"Oh, can we go to that new Asian place downtown? Lyra went there last Saturday. She loved it."

"And don't forget, our Fabulous Friday birthday dinner

will be in your honor, so pick the meal you'd like by tomorrow; I have time to go shopping for food. Pick your dessert, too."

"Really, Mom—you had to ask? You know I love carrot cake with cream cheese frosting, and I like it when we share different kinds of pizza. That's my favorite meal. What about Uncle Bill and Fr. Mike, are they going to be able to come?"

"Yes, sweetie, both of them said they would be here. There will be seven of us here for dinner on Friday."

Mom had said we could go shopping together on Saturday. Once that was decided, I was able to look forward to our Fabulous Friday dinner. Uncle Bill has always figured out a way to be invited to these meals, and lately, Fr. Mike has also been our guest. With all seven of us around the table it can be a little difficult to follow the different conversations. But it's so much fun, I wouldn't want it to be any other way.

Friday evening, six of us gathered around our dining room table. Everything was ready to eat. We kids were allowed to have a can of our favorite pop(soda) to go with the pizza. We were ready, but Fr. Mike hadn't arrived yet. We sat for 10 minutes, waiting for him to come. Mom put the pizza in the oven so we could give him another 10 minutes. We sat around doing what we do best:

Kevin: "What position does the ghost play in soccer?    A: The Ghoulie" ***

Mom: "Who helps the little pumpkins cross the road to school? A: The Crossing Gourd" ***

Dad: "What did the mother ghost tell her baby when she ate her ice cream too fast?
A: Quit goblin your dessert." ***

Katie: "Why did the witches stay in the Holiday hotel?
A: They heard it had good broom service." ***

Uncle Bill: "Why are ghosts such bad liars?
A: You can see right through them." ***

Gracie: "What is a vampire's favorite fruit?
A: Nectarines" ***

Just as Kevin was about to tell another joke, Fr. Mike came through the front door. "I'm sorry I'm late, but I had an emergency at the Urgent Care clinic. Ed Garrison—you know him, he's an usher at church—was in a car accident. His wife asked me to stop by and offer some support to him. He was lucky, only some minor cuts and bruises, but he did bump his head on the steering wheel, so he'll stay overnight for observation at the hospital in Riverview. What did I miss?"

"Only our amusing jokes. And, no, we won't repeat them."

"OK, so what if I tell my joke, I did come prepared."

"I'll get the pizza out of the oven while you tell your joke," said Becky.

"Ready? Here goes: "Why don't mummies go on vacation? A: They're afraid to relax and unwind." ***

"Could I tell one more, to make up for being late?" We all nodded "yes."

"Why can't skeletons play music at St. Brendan's? A: They have no organs." ***

"Ohhh", said Becky, as she set the two pizzas on the table, "that one's a groaner. *'Don't quit your day job,'* Fr. Mike, You'll never survive as a comedian."

Dinner on Friday was terrific; shopping with my mom and having lunch with both of my parents on Saturday was awesome. And at dinner on Saturday night, the twins gave me their gift: a toy hammock to hold my favorite dog, Toto, and my other stuffed animals.

"Wow, this is a great idea. I love it. Thanks, both of you." Dad said he would attach it to my bedroom wall.

My birthday was really special this year. I'm glad I'm still not **'sitting on the fence!'**


***Funnyeditor.com

# HONESTY IS THE BEST POLICY

## Becky and Uncle Bill

G reg's brother, the kids' uncle Bill, is one of our favorite people. He works at our kids' school as a guidance counselor (he helps kids when they have problems with other kids, sadness when someone they know dies, and is a resource person for the teachers.) He's calm, funny, and very understanding. So when I told him,

"We want to have you over for our Fabulous Friday dinner," I was surprised when he said,

"I'm not sure I'll be able to come."

I reminded him his birthday was coming up, and he would be the guest of honor. But he said, "I'll try to come. Please don't go to any trouble, in case I can't be there."

That evening, I talked to my husband, Greg, and told him about my conversation with his brother.

"Bill was very strange on the phone today. He wasn't his usual cheerful self. Do you think anything could be wrong? Wouldn't he tell us if something was bothering him? Doesn't he always tell the kids: **'Honesty is the Best Policy?'**"

Greg was unaware of anything that might be bothering Bill, but he promised to look in on him tomorrow at his office in the school. When he got there, the office was empty, so he went up to the principal's office to see if Mrs. Wileman had any idea of where Bill might be.

"I haven't seen him today. Come to think of it, I didn't see him yesterday, either. I figured he was spending the day at one of the schools in Riverview. Is there anything wrong?"

"No," I don't think so; I just wanted to check in with him. Thanks, Mrs. Wileman. Would you give me a call if he comes in today, please?"

"Of course," she told me.

A few hours later she called. "Bill came into the school today for a few minutes. He seemed very distracted, like something big was on his mind. He left before I could have a conversation with him."

"Thanks for calling me, I'm going to stop at his house and see if he's home."

I noticed Bill's car was in the driveway when I drove up and parked. I rang the bell, and it wasn't long before he opened the door.

"Greg, hi, what are you doing here?"

"May I come in, or do I have to stand on the porch?"

"It's not a good time, Greg. Maybe sometime later?"

"Are you OK, Bill?" You seem to be acting a little strange lately."

"Everything's fine, I just have a lot on my mind."

"Why don't you share what's going on?" I asked my brother.

"Nothing's wrong, really," Bill said.

"You never were a very good liar. Please tell me what's going on."

"I'm not ready to tell you. Please trust me to know what I'm doing."

"OK," I told him, but remember, **'honesty is the best policy.'** Lots of people love you and are concerned about you." I shook his hand, then turned and walked back to my car.

A week later, we still hadn't heard a word from Bill, which was very unusual. We called the school and were told by Mrs. Wileman that Bill had taken a few personal days and wouldn't be back until the weekend. She didn't think it was a medical problem or anything like that. Greg didn't think he was in any trouble with the law, which made both of us laugh because Bill always operates within the law. He's never even had a parking ticket—even Greg and I couldn't say that. The kids were beginning to ask why they hadn't seen their uncle lately.

"We usually see him around the school or at our house. We didn't even see him at church last weekend." Greg and I had to admit that we had no idea of what was going on with Bill.

On the following Sunday, Bill showed up at church. He seemed more relaxed and smiled when he saw all of us. During coffee and donuts, he told Greg and me that he needed to talk to us. He suggested a time in the afternoon. That was all he said, except to ask,

"How are the kids doing? I see they're still interested in donuts and orange juice."

Later that afternoon, we sent the kids to the movies so that we could sit and talk with Bill. Naturally, we were eager to hear what he had to say.

Becky began by saying, "Bill, we're worried sick about you. Are you OK? Is there something we need to know?"

"Yes, there is something you need to know, but it's not about me. It's about the munchkins."

"The munchkins? What about them?" Greg sounded like he was interrogating a suspect.

"I found their uncle. His name is Timothy Engel, and he lives in Virginia." He paused to let that piece of information sink in.

"How, Bill, how did you find him?" Becky was amazed and couldn't wait to know more.

"It WAS an amazing thing. I might even call it a miracle. Tim is the brother of Emma and Claire. He left home when he was 18 to get away from his abusive parents. He kept in contact with his sisters until both of them moved to Riverview. Then he lost contact with them. Unfortunately, he didn't know they had very young children. When he reached his late 20s, he tried to find his sisters. Unfortunately, it was after they had died in that car crash. Here's where the miracle comes in. He wrote to the Riverview Elementary School hoping to find out something about his sisters. The letter came to the principal, and after reading it, he gave it to me. It's a beautiful letter, in which he says he's been looking for his sisters—did the school know anything about them?"

"But what did he expect when he wrote that letter?" Becky asked.

"I think he was just trying to find some way to locate and renew his relationship with his sisters. I contacted him and gave him the bad news that his sisters had died in a car accident, but I wanted to get more information from him before I told him he was an Uncle. So I called him twice to talk and, finally, went to Virginia to meet him. That's why I was so preoccupied and distracted. I wanted to tell you everything as it happened, but I didn't want the kids to know in case this didn't work out. I didn't want them or you to be disappointed.

"As it turns out, he's a delightful person. He runs a small theater in his town. He has a hand in every phase of its operation. He loves to sing (sounds like Gracie,) he supervises the designing and sewing of costumes (reminded me of Katie,) and meets with a small crew to plan the building of the sets for each production (Kevin would love the hands-on work.) I think all of you will fall in love with him. He seems truly interested in having a relationship with the kids. They seem to be his only family members. With your permission, he would like to come to meet the kids and both of you. What do you think?"

"Wow, Bill, this isn't our usual coffee time without the kids. What do you think, Becky? Do you want to think about this news for a while?"

"You sound pretty sure that he's the munchkins' uncle and that he's a wonderful man. How do you feel about sharing your title 'Uncle' with someone else?" Becky needed to know how Bill felt. If he truly believed that **'honesty is the best policy,'** he would tell them exactly how he felt about this whole surprise event.

"After all these years, and the pain the kids suffered by the loss of their moms, I think it's great to have found a relative who seems very interested in getting to know them and to begin a serious relationship with them. I'm very excited to have him meet the kids. I hope the two of you feel the same. I would love to have another person join our family. Kids can't have too many uncles."

"I think it's awesome—like you said—a miracle. When could he come to meet all of us?" Greg looked at Becky, who nodded her head.

"How about if I invite him to come here for a few days next week? It's my birthday that weekend. I can't think of a better Fabulous Friday meal. I'll call him later and invite him."

"Please call us after you talk to him and let us know what he says." Becky couldn't hide the excitement in her voice.

After Bill left, the two of us sat for a long time, talking about this very unexpected news. For the most part, we are very happy about having the kids meet and get to know a very special relative. We hope they will find a connection to their moms through him.

"Who would have ever expected this?" Greg said in amazement.

On Fabulous Friday when we gathered to celebrate Bill's birthday, the kids seemed a little surprised to see a stranger at our dinner table, but they didn't say anything. Greg and I had spent an entire day with Tim and Bill while the kids were in school. It was just as Bill had told us. Tim Engel is a warm, humorous person with a genuine interest in getting to know his nieces and nephew. We had one of our usually crazy meals, with everyone contributing a joke. These seemed to have an animal theme:

Kevin: "What do you call the horse that lives
next door? A: Your neigh-bor." ***

Katie: "What animal floats best? A: A gir-raft." ***

Dad: "What dog likes to take bubble-baths?
A: A Shampoodle." ***

Bill: "Why did the unwashed chicken cross the road twice?
A: Because he was a dirty double-crosser." \*\*\*

Mom: "When is a black dog not a black dog?
A: When it's a greyhound." \*\*\*

Gracie: "What do bees say in the summer?
A: It's s-warm, isn't it?" \*\*\*

Even our guest jumped in with:
"Why couldn't the spring flower ride its bike?
A: It lost all its pedals." \*\*\*

When the laughter ended, we sang *Happy Birthday* to Bill and cut his cake. We gave him his gift from Greg and me. We had gotten him a putter to replace the old one he had bent from smacking it on the green so often. The kids got him a golf towel, a pack of balls, and a pad and pencil with a big eraser so he could keep track of his score. After he thanked all of us, he looked at Greg, Tim, and me and pushed his plate aside.

"I suppose you're wondering who our special guest is tonight. You all thought I was acting crazy for a long time now. That was because I was planning a huge surprise for the three of you. Katie, Gracie, Kevin, this is your uncle Tim. He is the brother of your moms, Emma and Claire. I'm going to let him tell you more."

"I feel a little nervous coming here like this. I guess it must be quite a shock for the three of you. I left home before you were born, and just recently was able to track you down by contacting the Riverview Elementary School to see if anyone there knew anything about your moms. Luckily, your uncle Bill received my letter and contacted me. I'm so sorry to hear about your moms' accident. I hope we'll be able to become good friends.

Gracie was the first to speak, "Are you really our moms' brother? Do you remember them?"

"Yes, honey, I remember them well. I grew up with them

until I moved away when I was 18. I moved around a lot and lost track of them."

"Are you going to be our uncle like Uncle Bill?" Kevin asked.

"I think your Uncle Bill is a very special man. I hope we'll all get to be good friends—family, even."

Katie couldn't think of anything to say, so she just got up from her chair, walked over to her uncle Tim and gave him a big hug.

"Looks like you're quickly becoming part of our family," I said.

Greg got up and shook Tim's hand. "Welcome to the family, Tim. You may want to start collecting jokes for our dinners."

As Greg, Bill and I cleaned up the table and washed the dishes, the three munchkins sat with Tim on the couch, telling him all the things they thought he should know about them:

"I like sports," said Kevin.

"So do I," said Tim, "especially baseball and football."

"I like to read," said Katie.

"Me, too." I like mysteries and books about traveling."

"I don't like Brussels sprouts," admitted Gracie.

"Neither do I," said her uncle Tim, shaking his head, "but I'm going to try to like them."

(Gracie looked more skeptical...)

*"Sounds like a match made in heaven,"* I thought, smiling at Greg, Bill and our three kids with their newfound relative.

***funnyeditor.com

# DON'T ATTACK THE MESSENGER

## Uncle Bill

Even though my job title is Guidance Counselor with the Riverview School District, which includes Rainbow Falls Elementary and the schools in Riverview, I occasionally will be asked to fill in for a teacher who has an emergency and no substitute teacher is available. Take this week for an example. Mr. Arnold, the sixth grade teacher's wife was going to was having a baby. Since babies don't plan their births ahead of time, no one knew exactly when Mr. Arnold would be needed at the hospital.

Today was THAT day! He called the principal, Mrs. Wileman, early in the morning, but there still wasn't enough time to contact a sub. So, I became the sub. I was able to reach Mr. Arnold at the hospital—he had a new baby daughter! He gave me some ideas for what to do in the classroom that morning. He thought he could come in after lunch.

I walked into the classroom feeling a little nervousness. I'm much better with kids one at a time or in a small group. Luckily, my nieces and nephew, Katie, Gracie, and Kevin, as well as many of their friends, would be in the room. I felt comfortable with them.

Probably my opening statement was not the best: "Mr. Arnold is out this morning, but he told me to give you the quiz he left on his desk. It's based on your history homework from yesterday." I may as well have said, "We're going to make you eat raw liver for lunch." Their response was immediate.

"A quiz? That's not fair. Mr. Arnold isn't even here. Why should we have to take a test when the teacher isn't even here?" The mood in the room seemed restless.

"Well, he'll be here this afternoon. You can tell him your complaints then. So please, **'Don't Attack the Messenger!'** I'm just telling you what he told me to say. You need to listen to the message without getting mad at the one who delivered it —in this case—me!" That gave them something to think about, and gave me a chance to plan my next strategy. "How many of you did your homework last night? Did you finish your history assignment?" A few people raised their hands, others looked down at their desks.

"OK, here's the plan. I'm going to give you the one hour before recess as a study time to make sure you know the history assignment well enough to ace the quiz. If you're confident you're prepared, then focus on some other subject, or read your library book. Just don't disturb the others."

After recess I gave them the quiz, and happily saw most kids finish the quiz quickly. Then we played a game I call, "What Would YOU Do?" I give them some possible situations and ask them how they would handle them. It's interesting to me to find out who looks at a problem and is able to separate feelings from the solution. For example, if someone tripped you on the playground, causing you to fall and scrape your hands, would you feel angry? Would your solution be to fight, talk things out, involve another person, or just walk away? Or let's say you broke something at home, would you tell your parents, hide the broken item, admit to what you did only if you were asked directly, or blame someone else?" Those who were willing to answer provided me with a look into a sixth-grader's mind.

When Mr. Arnold returned to his classroom after lunch, he seemed pleased at the results of the history quiz. He asked the class a few questions about spelling and ended the day with a spelling test. It was apparent afterward that the kids did a great job preparing for the history quiz, but went into the spelling test a little less prepared. In the end, the class had learned something valuable that morning: when you are faced with a new situation, you can feel angry, upset, afraid of failure, sorry, happy or grateful—how you handle it is a sign of growing up. Also, if a guidance counselor tells you there will be a test, **'don't attack the messenger!'**

# BARKING UP THE WRONG TREE

## Uncle Tim

J ust a couple months after the kids met their uncle Tim, and a few days before he was going back to Virginia after a short visit at our home, he had a glimpse of the trials of having children. He was sitting in the living room, reading the Sunday paper, when Katie and Kevin could be heard shouting upstairs.

"Give back my new comic book. It's mine. You had no right to go into my room and take it."

"I don't have your stupid comic book, and I was never in your room."

"Yes, you were. I saw you come out of my room. I saw you holding my new comic book."

"I'm telling you, Kevin, I don't have your comic book."

"Well, then where is it?" Kevin seemed confused.

Katie shouted, "I don't have your book, so leave me alone!"

Instead of keeping the noise upstairs, Kevin chased Katie down the stairs, through the kitchen and out the back door onto the lawn.

"Well, I suppose having them argue outside is better than having to listen to them in the house," said Uncle Tim.

He glanced over at Gracie, who was sitting on the couch reading a comic book.

"What are you reading, Gracie?"

"It's a comic book. We have a whole bunch of them upstairs in Kevin's room."

"Is that where you got this one?"

"Yes, it's the newest one he has. He bought it yesterday."

"So you're the one who *borrowed* his new comic book, not Katie."

"Please don't tell him. He'll be mad. I'm almost finished."

Soon after their conversation, Kevin chased Katie into the living room. Uncle Tim raised his voice to be heard over their shouting: "Sit down, the two of you, we have to talk."

Gracie didn't look too happy as she shoved the comic book under her legs.

"Kevin, I think you're **'Barking Up the Wrong Tree.'**"

"What do you mean, **'barking up the wrong tree?'**"

"It means that you're accusing the wrong person or looking in the wrong direction. Have you considered any other possibilities concerning your new comic book?"

"Do you mean that I should find out if someone else is to blame, not Katie?"

Suddenly, he turned to Gracie and said, "It was you, wasn't it?"

Gracie knew she was caught, so she quickly gave in. "Ok, I saw your new comic book lying on your dresser. I needed something to read, so I grabbed it when you were in your bathroom. Katie didn't take it. Honest, Kevin, I didn't think you would notice that it was missing before I had a chance to read it. I'm almost through, and I promise I won't tell you what's in it! I'm sorry you yelled at Katie because of what I did. Katie, it wasn't fair for you to get chased around the house and blamed for something I did. I'm sorry."

She pulled the comic book from under her legs and handed it to Kevin. He looked at his uncle and realized he needed to be the one to show forgiveness and not be angry.

"I'm sorry, I accused you, Katie. Gracie, you can finish the comic book. Please put it back on my dresser when you're through with it."

All would have been fine, but Gracie, remembered something her dad had said at another family "talk" a few weeks ago.

"Uncle Tim, you **'threw me under the bus'** when you told on me. That was tattling, but I guess I deserved it. I shouldn't have been sneaky."

Uncle Tim laughed. "You're right, Gracie. I shouldn't have turned you in to Kevin. Then he looked at the munchkins and said,

"You need to know how much I enjoy being with the three of you— silliness and all. Your parents have done a great job raising you. I think you'll be good for me. I hope I can be a part of this family for a long time." Then he chuckled and shook his head as he went back to reading his newspaper.

# DON'T BITE THE HAND THAT FEEDS YOU

## Uncle Bill

Every once in a while our kids will decide that nothing in their life is OK. They grumble and complain about everything. Greg and I just roll our eyes at each other and wait for the drama to end. This morning, much to our surprise, all three kids were in a snit. Nothing seemed to be going well for any of them.

It started at breakfast when Gracie complained, "I don't like this cereal. Why can't we have a choice?" I pointed out to her that she had chosen it when we went shopping this week.

Then Kevin told us: "Kids shouldn't have to do chores on Saturday, our free day from school." Again, I pointed out that each child has specific jobs to do.

"If you want to, you can do your chores on Wednesday afternoon or Monday evening or any other time that works, as long as your chores get done each week."

Greg and I waited for Katie to throw in her ideas about how the three of them are treated so terribly.

"We never get to do the things we want to do; we just have to listen to you. You don't know everything. Why do we have to listen to you?"

"Because I have the keys to your bike locks," said Greg. "Why don't you go for a little ride right now? You might want to go to the park, sit in the cement culvert and think about what you just told us."

When the kids left the garage on their bikes, Greg reached for his cell phone and speed-dialed his brother, Bill. Our kids have come to love him totally, so Greg thought perhaps he could walk through the park and "accidentally" find the kids sitting in the culvert. It's their favorite place to go when they're really upset with us. Bill said he had been working for a long time, so to stretch his legs on a little walk was just what he needed—he didn't know what a hornet's nest he might find in the park.

Bill:

When I reached the park, I did a quick scan to see if the kids were sitting around on the swings. As I looked toward the cement culvert, I could see several pairs of feet in the culvert and a few bodies connected to those feet. Acting on a strong hunch that the three Stewart munchkins were inside their favorite place, I walked straight toward them and stuck my head into the culvert. The echo as I talked was amazing. Without being invited, I scooted into the end of the culvert and stretched my long legs outside on the grass. The first thing I noticed was the sullen, unhappy look on all three kids. It was then that I realized I had said, "Yes, I'll take a walk over there," having no idea of what I might find *over there*.

"What's going on? You look miserable. Do you want to talk about it?" Well, if the kids' anger was a fire hose, I would have been soaked in just a few seconds. All their disappointment, disapproval and unfairness of life with their parents came pouring out. No part of their lives was left unchallenged.

"Our mom and dad are so unfair, Uncle Bill. Their rules are harsh, and they always seem to be unhappy with what we do," said Katie. The other two nodded their heads in agreement.

I listened quietly before speaking. "It's hard to be your age. You want freedom, but I'll bet you also want your parents there when you need a hug or some good advice and support. Am I right?" This time all three of them reluctantly mumbled, "Yes."

"I want the three of you to come up with two things each of you dislike about living with your parents." I paused while the kids decided what to tell me.

"Mom and Dad won't let us do things we want to do, like buy our own clothes. They won't even let us have pop (soda) when we're watching TV or with lunch or dinner." That was Gracie's contribution.

"They make us do chores when we have other plans. They expect us to keep our rooms clean." That came from Kevin.

"OK, Katie, what about you? What bugs you about your mom and dad?" I wanted to know more, although I had a pretty good idea of where this whole conversation was going.

"I want to pick my own bedtime so I can read for as long as I want. Our parents are too strict; there are too many rules."

"That was very informative. I had no idea life is so difficult for each of you. Now, to be fair, I want you to think of two things your parents have done for you that was good, kind, or helpful." Once again, I paused to give the kids time to think.

Katie went first. "They adopted us and let us live in their house."

Kevin said, "Dad taught me to play catch and lets me help him build things in the garage."

Gracie had to admit, "They're good cooks. There's always enough food, and both Mom and Dad will listen if we have a problem."

"Think about everything you just said. Which list is more important to you? Are your parents kind, compassionate, helpful, caring, fair? Are they helping each of you to become the best person you can be, or are they just grumpy, unfair people who have too many rules and don't seem to really care about you?"

There was a little bit of sighing and wiggling before the munchkins admitted that their parents were more good than bad.

"You know, there's a saying: **'Don't Bite the Hand That Feeds You.'** Think about all the ways your parents show you that they love you so much. Then, think about the ways that you spend your time being whiny and full of complaints. I think all the negative things you said about your parents can seem disrespectful and hurtful to them, so be careful when you talk to your mom and dad about how you feel. Be willing to listen to their explanation of what they see as their responsibility as parents raising three active and somewhat challenging children."

I smiled after I said that. "Considering all the things you said just now, I think the three of you are very lucky. I know your parents—they are two awesome people who will love you no matter what you do. Don't take advantage of that. **'don't bite the hand that feeds you.'** Now, I need to get back to my very boring paperwork. It was nice to see all of you again. Please go home and tell your parents how much I appreciated their phone call." *They'll know what I mean!*

# GET DOWN TO BRASS TACKS

## Mr. Arnold

I've been the sixth grade teacher for several months now, and I have to say that I'm pretty impressed with my class. They work hard, seem to get along well, are helpful, dependable, and friendly. I've seen a few leaders emerge from the group, and have recognized those who need help to get started. Since we had a small group activity coming up, I spent some time working on which kids would be in each group. I hoped to have each group have a strong leader—a kid who would work hard and stay focused, and at least one kid in each group who needed some support to get the work done.

"OK, kids, we've been working on famous people and events that have been important to the formation of this country. I'm going to divide you into five groups—four people to a group. I tried to mix you up so that you might be in a group with people who are not your favorite friends.

"Each group will have to come up with a character or an event from our American history class, do research into who the person or event was, what the person or event did for our country. What were the problems that were faced? How is that person or event remembered in today's society? Do you have any questions?"

"How long do we have to work on this project? Do we work on it in class only? Will we make just one report? Will each of us get the same grade?"

"The answer to all of your questions is, 'Yes.'" For the next two weeks, I'll give your group 30 minutes at the end of the day to talk about the information you found. At the end, you will have to agree as to what information will go into your final report. Each of you will hand in the final copy of your part of the report. All those pages will be your entire project. I'll collect them on that Friday.

"OK, because this is history class time, you may talk in your group to select a topic, decide who will research one section of the project and make a statement as to what you have chosen to study and why. Now, you have 15 minutes to chat with each other and share ideas. I expect you to **'Get Down to Brass Tacks'**—that means you have several important decisions to make right now. You have lots to do. Focus, focus, focus. And don't waste your time."

The topics they decided upon after about 20 minutes of arguing and talking in loud whispers were:

Gracie: "So do we agree that we want to do our report on Paul Revere and his importance to the American Revolution?"

Mary: "I think we have the perfect event: the Pilgrims' coming to America and landing at Plymouth Rock."

Jamie: "This is going to be fun: the writing of the Declaration of Independence."

Tommy: "Our class will love our report on Benjamin Franklin and his work on electricity and eyeglass lenses."

Lyra: "I'm glad it didn't take us too long to decide on 'how the Native Americans helped the new colonists.'"

Two weeks later I sat at my desk and listened to five reports. Each one amazed me. They were well-researched, covered all the necessary information, involved all the kids in the group, and provided a fairly polished report. It was clear to me that some members worked harder than others, a thing common in every work group, but the s did a great job of keeping everyone active. Each group spent a lot of time deciding what was important for the rest of the class to know.

I think they were very proud of their finished project.

I might consider having a few other "team projects" in other subjects. I enjoyed the free time I had to do other things at my desk while they were working, although several times each day, someone would come to me to ask my advice on a problem they couldn't solve as a group. I must admit that even though I got a lot of work done during their group time, once the projects were finished and turned in, I had to **'get down to brass tacks,'** read all their papers, and give them comments and a grade—there goes my weekend!!

# A WORD TO THE WISE IS ENOUGH

## Greg and Becky

Tonight at supper, Becky and I watched our kids act in a way that was probably appropriate for their age (eleven), but it drove us crazy. Gracie had come home from school a little later than usual, and the twins were watching TV just before the three of them headed to the dining room table. The twins were very giggly and making strange noises. We all sat down, said a prayer like we always do; that's when the foolishness started:

"Gracie has a boyfriend. Gracie has a boyfriend!"

"No, I don't!" Gracie shouted at them.

"Yes, she does, Mom. We saw them playing tetherball after school. They were laughing. Gracie has a boyfriend!" Kevin loves taunting his sister.

"Just because Gracie was playing tetherball with a boy doesn't mean that she has a boyfriend, unless you're saying she has a friend and he happens to be a boy," suggested Mom.

"He's just a kid I met after school. He was waiting for his dad to pick him up. I like playing tetherball and so does he." Gracie sounded a little defensive.

"Gracie has a boyfriend. Gracie has a boyfriend," the twins kept on taunting her.

"Sounds like Gracie made a new friend this afternoon. That's no reason to tease her. Please stop, so that we can pay attention to our meal," suggested Dad.

Unfortunately, the twins had gotten stuck in teasing mode, and they continued, "Gracie has a boyfriend." Then they added kissing sounds. It clearly made her angry. Again, we told the kids to pay attention to their food and stop shouting. However, it wasn't surprising that this whole behavior got worse in another way. The kids began to kick each other under the table while wiggling and giggling, with Gracie glaring at them.

Once more Becky told them, "Last warning: STOP!" Even though she said that very sternly, it was clear to me that her words had no effect on the kids, especially when I got kicked in the ankle by a wild foot that hit the wrong target. Having reached the end of my patience, I let them know that by declaring: "OK,THAT'S IT!I want the three of you to follow me into the living room. Kevin and Katie, you sit on the floor leaning against the couch. Gracie, you sit on the floor with your back against the footstool." I pushed the footstool forward so that she was sitting very close to the twins with her legs straight ahead between her sister and brother.

As soon as they were all settled in, I told them to join hands in a circle. "Now, I want the three of you to sit here holding hands for 15 minutes. If you struggle, lose your grip on a hand, or talk, your mom and I will add another 15 minutes. If you manage to go 15 minutes with no problem, you can join us for dessert. Otherwise, it may be that you'll be 12 years old before you can let go of each other's hands! **'A Word to the Wise is Enough.'"**

Our kids are very quick to catch on to 'the wise' you might say, so for 15 minutes, our three munchkins managed to sit holding hands quietly and without a struggle. Finally, Becky walked up to them and said, "You did very well. Now, for five minutes we want you to sit normally—no need to hold hands—while you talk to each other as respectful, kind, and loving kids who happen to be related to each other . . . apologize if you must, then you may join us for dessert."

We had a wonderful, quiet, polite dessert and were very happy with the three of them, until they went up to their rooms. Then we heard "Gracie has a boyfriend, Gracie has a boyfriend!" start all over again. Evidently, **'a word to the wise is enough'** for less than 30 minutes.

# PRACTICE WHAT YOU PREACH

## The Stewart Family

For most of our married life, Greg has wanted to be a police officer and then a detective. He studied very hard for the detective's exam and passed with flying colors. We were all so proud of him. Katie, Kevin and Gracie joined our family after he had become a detective, but our two married children had been very excited to attend his promotion ceremony when they were young.

The three munchkins think he has the most interesting job—ever! They were surprised, when he announced at dinner last night, that he was thinking of applying for another job. Captain Terry Gallagher, who has been the Chief in charge of the entire Rainbow Falls and Riverview Police Department, announced that she was retiring in four months. Greg admitted that he had never been in charge of a large group of people before, but he knew everyone on the force and understood their jobs, since he has been working at the same job for many years.

"Are you going to apply for the job?" asked Kevin, hoping he would get into less trouble with his dad if his dad was the Chief of Police.

"Yes, I'm thinking about it, and no, you wouldn't get into less trouble if I was the Chief."

*"How does he do that? Sometimes, he reads my mind!"*

Katie wanted to know: "Would you still be Mr. Stewart? Or would we call you 'Chief Stewart' or 'Mr. Chief Stewart?' Could we still call you 'Dad?'"

"I would never take a job that meant you couldn't call me 'Dad.' That's my favorite title. I suppose others would call me 'Chief Stewart,' or 'Captain Stewart,' if the job comes with a promotion. But I haven't decided yet to try for the job, so don't worry about what changes a new job might mean.

Later that night, Becky asked me, "Are you serious about applying for this job?" Becky seemed a little concerned. "I imagine there will be other candidates. Will there be a lot of competition for the position, and how might it affect your life here at home with me and the munchkins?"

"Those are great questions, Becky, and I promise we'll talk about all possible details once I know them myself. I imagine there will be some sort of job description coming out soon."

"OK, honey, you know I'll support you no matter what you choose to do."

"Thanks, sweetheart, that's good to know."

About a week later the job description for Riverview and Rainbow Falls Chief of Police was posted. Dad got a copy and brought it home so that all of us could look at it. He took the time to tell us about the job during supper that night.

"I looked this over yesterday and today and saw the regular things I expected: to plan and direct all activities of the police department. Also, I would have to meet with reporters and members of the public. I would be responsible to the mayors and council members of Rainbow Falls and Riverview. You all know Mayor Sarah Williams. She would be my boss."

"What do you have to do to apply for this position, Dad?"

"Good question, Gracie. I would have to take a written test, undergo some testing to see if I have the right personality for this job, I'd have to meet with a search committee who would ask lots of questions and answer any questions I might have. I feel pretty confident of doing all the tasks they require, except for the office management and public activities. I've had little experience doing that."

"You have to take a test, Dad? Good luck with that." (Katie hated tests).

"Thanks for all your faith in me, sweetie; I'll study and try to do my best. That's all your mom and I expect from you, too."

"You know, Dad, do you remember when we were thinking of starting our doggy washing job? We made a list of reasons to do the job or not do it. You could make two lists like that. Our lists helped us to make the right decision, I'll bet it would help you, too."

"That's an excellent idea, Kevin. I may even ask the rest of you if you have any suggestion for either list."

"I think I need to spend time thinking about this position and talk with your mom and Uncle Bill. If we decide I should move forward, I would need to study for the test. Now I know how you kids feel!"

Greg was really serious about this possible job change. He spent time by himself, consulted with his brother, Bill, and talked the most with me. We made two lists, like Gracie suggested; we looked them over for several days. One night we gave the lists to the kids to examine. They were pretty simple to understand:

Reasons for TAKING the job

--It will be a new challenge.
--I can use most of the skills I already have.
--I enjoy and respect all the people I would continue
   to work with.
--I think many people in the Rainbow Falls and Riverview
   communities know and respect me.
--I want to make these towns places where people
   feel  safe and cared about.
--It would be a step up in my career and may include
   a  raise in salary and other benefits.
--It would mean that my children would ALWAYS have
   to call me "**Sir**!"

Reasons for NOT TAKING the job

--It would be like being a new teacher going into

sixth grade and having to learn new things that
  might  make  me uncomfortable
--Maybe some of the other officers will think I'm
  'showing off.'
--I might have less time with my family.
--I like to work at home whenever possible. I don't
  know  if I want to give that up.
--There will be more night meetings—attending
   public events, working on committees,
   consulting  with the Mayors.
--Sometimes bigger positions change people. They
   find themselves loving the power.

"Gosh, Dad, you did a great job with these," said Kevin. "If you get the job, would you have a cool uniform with some fancy pins on it? You'll probably get a neat new badge. Do you think we could keep your old badge?"

"Sorry, Kevin, but I've already seen the prank you pulled with my badge. I'll turn it in or lock it in my safe!"

"I'm concerned about the amount of time you may have to spend at work. Will your home life suffer?" Mom asked.

"That's also a big concern of mine, honey. I promise we'll consider that together."

Bill wanted to know: "Do you think you have the ability to think quickly when someone on a committee or a reporter asks a question? If you get the job, I think you may feel rushed to make decisions, when you really prefer to have some time to think things over." (My brother probably knows me better than anyone when it comes to making decisions.)

"Thanks, Bill, that's a helpful insight."

Later that night, when Becky and I got ready for bed, she asked me if I was close to making a decision. I remember her telling me she would support me no matter which choice I made. So, I asked her,

"What are your ideas, Becky? Do you think I can handle this

possible new job?"

"I think you can do anything you decide to do. You're a hard worker. The question is, will this job make you happier than you are now? That's the question you have to answer—when you look at your lists, which one will make you happier?"

"You know, Bill asked me the same thing, so I guess I need to spend some time thinking about that. But no more tonight, I need to think about something else or better yet, someone else. How was your day today? Are you at all anxious over this job search and how it might change our family?"

"I always worry about our family. If you decide to go for this job and it changes life around here, we'll adjust and figure out a way to make our family life be as good as it is now."

*I love my wife because she's always so positive.*

A few days later, I announced that I was going to apply for the new position. That didn't mean I would get the job or would decide to take it if it was offered to me. I guess I wanted the challenge to see if I could do it.

The first thing I had to do was take a written test on police procedures. Luckily, I had three kids who couldn't wait to offer their advice:

"You know, Dad, you always tell us to study, study, study before a big test. We think you should do the same thing —**'Practice What You Preach,'** Dad— No TV, no distractions, just one good hour of studying every night for the next week."

"Wow, you are tough supervisors. I'll do my best."

Katie told him, "And just remember the three words that will help you out while you're studying: "GO ASK MOM!" The kids laughed, but Becky rolled her eyes to the ceiling.

For the next five nights, Greg was in his office reading and studying a sample test. He was unavailable to everyone unless it was an emergency. On the day of the test, he was a little nervous but felt that he was as prepared as he could be. At dinner, he announced to us:

"I passed! I did the best I could on every question. A few questions made me stop and think for a little while, but I finished within the time limit. I'm so relieved!" He looked more relaxed than he did in the morning.

"I think this calls for a celebration—ice cream for everyone tonight!" Becky declared, and no one objected!

Two days later, I went through a meeting with a special doctor to see if I had the ability to handle the anxiety and stress that might come with the job. The doctor wanted to know if I had any reason to believe I might not be a good match for the job.

"Truthfully," I said to her, "I'm a little anxious about changing jobs, but I'm sure that I would quickly adjust to the demands of the office of Chief of Police."

After going through that meeting, I had to meet with several representatives from the police departments, the public (including a few reporters) and a private meeting with the Mayors. At the end of this part of the selection process, I was exhausted and glad I was finished. Now, all I had to do was wait to see who would be selected to be Chief of Police.

While he waited, Greg talked to his brother and me about how difficult the entire process had been. Greg asked us if we thought he could handle the job. Both of us said we were sure he could grow into the job. But Bill suggested: "Let's go back to the two lists you made. When you think of this new job possibility and the work you have now, which one do you think will make you the happiest? Remember the saying, *'If you love the job you have, you'll never work a day in your life.'*"

"As for me, I told you already that I will support you no matter what your position is in the police department," Becky reminded him.

"Thanks, Becky, knowing that takes away a lot of pressure and worry. I love you. And, yes, I love you, too, Bill. Your opinion always means a lot to me. Guess all we have to do now is wait."

The time seemed to drag. Then this morning, I was called into the Rainbow Falls Mayor's office. She began by saying that I had done very well throughout the whole interviewing process. I kept waiting for the "but . . ." Finally it came:

"This was a very difficult choice. You were a very strong candidate, Greg, but, in the end, it came down to someone who had more experience with police work AND the management skills required for this high profile job. I would have enjoyed working with you; however, I think you and I will find that Jack Robinson will be an excellent Chief."

This afternoon, Greg came home and told me of the Mayors' and search committees' decision.

"How are you feeling, honey? Are you happy, sad, sorry, relieved?"

"I'm feeling several things, most of them you just mentioned, but in some ways I feel like a failure, or as Kevin used to say, 'A loser.' Did I let you down?"

"I would never think of you as a loser or a failure. Someone with more experience with the public was chosen over you. It's not your fault for not having a skill that's not needed in your job now. You heard her say that you were a finalist. That's great. The kids will be so proud of you. Of course, you didn't let us down."

Dinner this evening began very quietly, as Bill and the kids waited to hear the news. Who would be the next Chief of Police? However, with three kids at the table, seriousness never lasted long.

Kevin: "What did Baby corn ask Mama corn?
A: Where is Pop corn?" ***

Gracie: "Why was the snake coughing so much?
A: He had a frog in his throat." ***

Katie: "What happened when a dog swallowed a

clock?  A: It got ticks." ***

After the three adults finished groaning, Dad coughed to get our attention, but Gracie asked, "Dad, do you have a frog in your throat?" That made everyone laugh.

"I thought you might like to hear the results of the job search I did." Everyone got very quiet. "I was a strong finalist, but the Mayors and Councils of each town decided to hire a man who has more experience dealing with: the public, reporters, and with conflicts that are sure to come up with the town councils. I hope you aren't disappointed in me; I really did try my best. I'm going to support Jack Robinson as the new Chief. I hope he becomes a good friend and co-worker."

"You are the greatest role model ever, Dad, not only did you **'practice what you preach,'** but you showed us how to be a positive person, even when you didn't get the job," said Kevin.

"We're proud of you, Dad—way to go!" Katie clapped her hands. We all joined in. Gracie jumped up and kissed her dad. Kevin and Katie did, too. As I hugged Greg, Bill walked up to his brother.

"Are you going to hug me, too?" asked Greg, warily.

"No way," said Bill, as he fist bumped him and clapped him on the shoulder. "Proud to have you as my brother."

My husband is the most wonderful person. We're glad he will remain a detective. He already has a very good, challenging job, and it comes with lots of time to spend with his family. Can't get much better than that!

***funnyeditor.com

# THE STRAW THAT BROKE
# THE CAMEL'S BACK

## Becky

"OK," I said as I came down the stairs waving a pair of muddy shoes that belonged to Kevin. "Enough is enough." I held up the shoes. "We have a mat at each door for shoes to sit when no one's wearing them, especially dirty ones. This is **'The Straw That Broke the Camel's Back.'** He's piled up too many chores that I end up doing. A camel may be able to carry a huge pile of straw, but finally, there's one straw that makes him collapse. I've run out of patience with Kevin. I'm tired of cleaning up after him, Greg. Go look at his room. There are dirty dishes, an empty yogurt container, a few napkins, a glass with orange juice in it, and a bed that hasn't been made in a week. We have a son who is living like a barnyard animal. His clean clothes are thrown into the closet, while the hangers are empty. His wastebasket is full of crushed, round pieces of paper looking suspiciously like little basketballs."

Just to please me, Greg came upstairs and looked into Kevin's room.

"You missed the library book and homework folder in his bathroom, and I might as well mention the towels on the floor. His laundry basket looks good—but that's because it's empty.

"This weekend, I'm going to spend time with him helping him to clean out and clean up his room. We'll get it in good shape, and then, if something like this happens again, I'll remind him of his responsibility for his things, and then I'll confiscate one item in his room each day. Soon he may find that the things he likes or needs are disappearing. There will be some sort of consequence to get an item back."

"That sounds like a reasonable plan, but it may cause you more work than you anticipated. Remember the saying, **'When the Rubber Hits the Road?'** Things that sound good in our minds, don't always work out so well when they're put into practice. But it's worth a try. I'll support whatever you decide to do."

Bright and early, I was up and ready to tackle my son's messy room. He was just finishing his breakfast when I approached him and said, "I hope you don't have any plans for this morning because you are mine for the next two hours."

He looked at me with a bewildered look on his face.

"Why, I haven't done anything wrong. What are we going to do?""

"Let's go up to your room, for starters. We'll move on from there," I said.

When we stopped at the doorway to his room, I asked him, "What do you see when you look into your bedroom?"

"I see my bed and dresser, the window, the closet and the floor."

"Can you really see the floor? From here, I see all kinds of different things—a jacket and the clothes you wore to church last Sunday laying on the floor. There are food items on the dresser and under the bed. Your clothes in the closet have just been tossed in there—the hangers are empty. The blinds are still closed, and the bed is unmade. And let's not even mention the homework folder and library book sitting on the counter in your bathroom. There's even a pen sitting in the sink. Your wastebasket is full of paper balls. I'm guessing that some of those cleared the rim of the wastebasket, and some hit the wall before falling into the basket. How can you live like this, Kevin? Is this part of your plan to drive me crazy?"

"Gosh, Mom, I don't even notice this stuff. I just kick stuff on the floor out of my way. My homework folder goes to school with me every day. On the weekend, it likes hanging out in the bathroom with my library book." He smiled. I did not.

"OK, we're going to clean out this mess and straighten up the closet. First thing: empty your wastebasket, we're going to need to fill it with other things. No stopping to talk to ANYONE."

It didn't take him too long to accomplish that task, so we moved on to the next one. "Now make your bed." I watched him as he struggled with the top sheet.

I tried to give him a clue. "Use both sides of the bed. Straighten one side, then the other." That seemed to help.

"Good job, now pick up all the things that are related to food and take them downstairs to the kitchen. Use your empty wastebasket to carry things. Throw away the trash, rinse the dishes and leave them in the sink. Then come back—don't get sidetracked."

"What does 'sidetracked' mean?"

"It means getting distracted and forgetting what you're supposed to be doing. You're pretty good at that, kiddo".

While he was gone, I took the time to look into his bathroom. As Greg had said, there was his library book he couldn't find last week and a homework folder that, luckily, didn't contain any overdue assignments. There were a few towels on the floor or hanging on the bar above the bathtub. His pajamas were under the library book.

"Your room is looking better. Now, go after all the clean clothes in your closet that should be hung up. I'm going downstairs to see what the rest of the family is doing."

The girls had gone off on their bikes to meet some friends, and Greg was in the garage pretending he knew how to fix our broken toaster.

"Why don't you just go down to the bank and open a savings account? They'll give you a new toaster as a gift."

"No way, it can't be too hard to fix this; it's just a small appliance."

"OK, if you say so . . . I'm going back to supervise the cleaning of Kevin's room. He's on the second last part."

When I returned to Kevin's room, he was still picking up

clothes and hanging them in his closet, but his room has taken on a whole new look. (Not that he likes it, but I do.)

"That's it, Mom, all my clothes are off the floor."

"Bring your folder and library book into your bedroom and put them on your desk. All your dirty clothes and towels should be in the hamper in the bathroom." Then I told him his final task:

"All right, munchkin, your room is finally looking livable. Now all you have to do is vacuum the floor, especially under the bed. There are some dust bunnies down there that seem to be multiplying."

When he was finished, his room looked great. It was neat and clean, and everything was in its place. Even his pajamas were back on his bed. I asked him,

"Doesn't this look and feel better?"

"It's OK, but, honestly, I like the *old* look better."

That evening, after the kids had gone to bed, Greg asked me, "Did you tell Kevin you are going to take something away from him every time you think his room is too messy?"

"No, I gave in on that. With the condition his room might be in, my taking an item out of it will not even be noticed. Yes, his room might get neater from having fewer treasures in it, but our room would get crowded with all of his stuff piled in here. You were right—a plan that sounds good doesn't always work **'when the rubber hits the road.'"**

(*The same thing could be said about Greg's great plan to fix the toaster. It hit a snag. A brand new toaster appeared on our kitchen counter on Monday. When our next bank statement comes in the mail, I'll bet there will be a new Christmas savings account, opened by Greg Stewart, for $5.*)

# DON'T BEAT AROUND THE BUSH

## Bill Stewart and Jake

I'm the counselor in both Riverview and Rainbow Falls Elementary Schools. It's commonly known that I have an "everyone's welcome" policy for all the students, teachers, staff, and parents.

Today, at 3:30 p.m., as I was sitting at my desk in Rainbow Falls, there was a knock at my door. When I got up and opened the door, I found Jake, the boy who had moved here from Germany before fifth grade, standing there. I invited him in. He seemed a little uncomfortable, so I asked, "Would you like a cookie, Jake?" (Cookies are known to comfort kids when they're upset.) Jake looked anxious. His eyes searched the room as if he was looking for a way to escape if he decided coming to see me was a bad idea. He said "No, thanks" to the cookie.

"Is everything OK, Jake, you seem a little nervous. Are you OK? How can I help you?"

"I'm OK, Mr. Stewart. I was just wondering if I could talk to you about something." He began to rub his hands as he looked down at his lap while he continued: "I don't know what to do, I mean, I don't want to get anyone into trouble. I don't want to make anyone mad at me. It might just be nothing."

"Jake, please stop. **'Don't Beat Around the Bush.'** Just tell me why you're here. Obviously you're really concerned about something that's bothering you a lot. Take a deep breath and tell me why you're here."

"I saw something happen today. I don't know if it was a bad thing or not. I don't want to say anything to Mr. Arnold if it means someone might get into trouble, but, if it was a bad thing, Mr. Arnold needs to know. What should I do?

"Kiddo, you still haven't told me exactly why you're here.

What did you see?"

"I was in our classroom after school, in the closet that contains our artwork. I was getting a picture I drew today. I was just about to walk back into the room when I saw Avalon, that"s a girl in my class, go into Mr. Arnold's desk and take out the envelope that has our Holiday savings money in it. We had just put in our monthly donations this morning. Mr. Arnold takes it to the bank and puts it into our class account. I guess he didn't lock the drawer. Avalon put the envelope in her jacket pocket and left the room. I don't want to tell on her if she wasn't doing anything wrong, but if she did, then who should I tell?"

"Has Mr. Arnold ever left that drawer open before?"

"I don't think so, he's pretty careful about our money."

"Tell me what you know about Avalon. Is she a nice person? Is she someone you trust? Has she done anything to make you think she would steal?" I hoped he could give me a better picture of this girl. I hadn't had any contact with her this year.

"I don't know her very well. She's very quiet. Sometimes Gracie and Katie eat lunch with her. She's pretty smart."

"Well, here's what I suggest. Tomorrow, you and I can meet at the school at 8:30 a.m. in Mrs. Wileman's office. I'll ask her to get Mr. Arnold to join us. You can tell them what you saw so we can get closer to the truth. OK? Are you all right with doing that?"

"OK, I won't get into any trouble, will I? I don't want to get Avalon in trouble, either."

"Let's take this one step at a time, Jake. See you tomorrow. Thanks for coming here. I'm glad you thought you could trust me."

"Kevin has told me about how you've helped him out of all kinds of trouble, so I hoped you could help me, too."

"You aren't in any trouble, Jake, so don't worry about it tonight." I walked him to the door and watched him head for his bike and ride away.

The next morning, Jake showed up in the principal's office right on time. Principal Wileman was there, as well as Mr. Arnold and me. He had that scared look on his face, again, so I reminded him that he wasn't in any trouble. He seemed to relax just a bit.

"Jake, would you tell Mr. Arnold and Mrs. Wileman what you saw yesterday afternoon in your classroom? Just give them the facts as you told them to me."

Jake took a deep breath and said, "I was in our closet getting my art project. I saw Avalon come into the room, open one of your desk drawers, Mr. Arnold, and take the envelope with our Holiday money. She put it in her pocket and left. I don't know where she went." He looked at Mr. Arnold and then at the floor.

"I don't want to get anyone into trouble, but I don't want to lose our money, either," he said quietly.

"Thank you, Jake, for your courage and desire to know the truth. I think I can help you with that. I was in a hurry yesterday and had carried a huge pile of papers to my car, when I realized I needed to go the bank with our money. I didn't have time to put the papers carefully into the car and run back to my classroom, so when I saw Avalon, I asked her to hurry to the classroom and get the envelope. I gave her the key to the drawer. So you can relax, kiddo, everything is fine. I put the money in the bank on my way home."

"Oh, I'm so glad. I didn't want to get Avalon into trouble."

"'We'd better hurry to get to our class—it's time for history," said Mr. Arnold as he put his hand on Jake's back and steered him toward the door.

"Today certainly was better than yesterday afternoon," I remarked to Mrs. Wileman. "Then I had to tell him, **'don't beat around the bush.'** Just now he was clear and direct—what a nice change."

"Amen to that," said Mrs. Wileman.

# TWO WRONGS DON'T MAKE A RIGHT

## Fr. Mike

T his year, just before Winter Break and all the excitement of the Holidays, there was an incident at the park that needed some adult intervention. Since I happened to be walking past the park when the attack was being planned, I couldn't help but get involved.

I saw a large group of girls standing in a circle, obviously planning something big. Since I recognized several of the girls, Katie and Gracie being two of them, I greeted all of them and asked what the big meeting was about.

"You all look so serious, are you planning the overthrow of the government?"

"No, Fr. Mike," said, Katie, "we're just getting even with the boys. Yesterday we were ice-skating on the pond when the boys came and threw snowballs at us. It was hard to skate and dodge snowballs, too. It's lucky none of us got hurt." The other girls nodded their heads in agreement.

"So, are you planning a counter-attack? Are you going to launch snowballs onto the ice while the boys are playing Capture the Flag?"

"Yes, it's going to be so sweet—they won't expect anything. We have the snowballs hidden in a snow bank at the edge of the pond." Gracie said with glee.

"Yeah," said a girl I didn't know. "They're going to be really surprised."

The boys were just beginning to skate. The flags were planted in the snow at each end of the pond. The girls began to get excited. Just as they were going to head to the snowball pile, I decided I needed to intervene.

"I know you're looking forward to pelting the

boys with snowballs to get back at them for doing that to you, but I think you would all agree that what they did was wrong. Otherwise, you wouldn't be planning your revenge. That's what it is, you know, revenge. They did something wrong, now you plan to do something equally wrong. It may feel satisfying, but **'Two Wrongs Don't Make a Right.'** And, in addition to that, how would you feel if someone got hurt? Would you let one of the boys hurt one of you to get even?"

"Well, I guess not," admitted CeCe, Katie's good friend.

"I have an idea. Are all of you pretty good skaters? Would you say you were as good as the boys?"

"You bet we're as good as the boys. They might be stronger, but we're faster and can turn quicker," said another girl I didn't know. Again, they all nodded in agreement.

Before the guys got too far into their game, I called them over to where the girls were standing. Everyone looked either annoyed or surprised. I took a deep breath and hoped I was doing the right thing.

"I understand that yesterday you boys ruined the girls' skating time by throwing snowballs at them. Is that correct?"

"Yes, sir," said one of the boys who probably didn't know I was a priest.

"It was just supposed to be a joke. No one got hurt, Fr. Mike," said Kevin, trying to justify what they did.

"I'm sure you thought it was just a joke, but did you know that the girls have planned to retaliate—to get even—with you? I've already talked to them about how **'two wrongs don't make a right,'** so their plan is really not acceptable. I'm sure all you boys agree with that—right?"

Again, I saw a bunch of heads nodding in agreement.

"Here's something that might work. Why don't you all play Capture the Flag? The girls have accepted the challenge of skating with all of you. Can you take on the challenge of working on a team that has both boys and girls? You might have to make some adjustments, but it seems like the only way to avoid an all-out-war. Are you willing to try it? If it doesn't seem to be working out, just remember that the girls have hidden a huge pile of snowballs, and they're eager to use them. Give it your best attempt, guys. I think you'll have lots of fun. Do you all know each other? (Heads shaking "no") You might start by introducing yourselves, so you won't be strangers for long. Good luck—I know you can do it."

As I watched all of them run to the ice, the boys had to wait for the girls to get on their skates, but they didn't seem impatient. They went around the pond a few times, no doubt getting rid of some excess energy. After a brief explanation of the rules, a rather spirited game began.

As I walked toward my house I thought: **'two wrongs don't make a right,'** *but two wrongs can lead to a right if both sides are willing.*

# DON'T COUNT YOUR CHICKENS BEFORE THEY'RE HATCHED

## Greg and Becky

This year, as in most years, the Christmas season begins after Thanksgiving (or even sooner) with the commercials about toys and other gifts, the movies that save ski resorts and inns from being sold to companies that want to make them into condos and huge shopping malls, and the people who find a love they thought would never happen. We try to keep our kids from getting all caught up in the shopping fever, but we do allow them to post a list of three things they might want (I said 'want' not 'need'!). This year we are prepared to have all three of them ask for cell phones. Santa might grant their wish on this one.

My husband mentioned, after it started getting cold, that he thought he might like to try golfing next spring. He has a few friends on the police force and several neighbors who go golfing on the weekends or sometimes in the early morning or late afternoon. He hinted that he needed golf clubs (a putter, a driver, and a wedge plus some other stuff that golfers need.) He didn't send a lot of hints into the air toward me, but I had a hunch he was expecting that the only wish on his list would be granted. The kids were being unusually quiet in the house, polite, helpful and hard working at both their chores and homework. Some times it is the most wonderful time of the year!

Kevin, Gracie and Katie were each given $25 to spend on the other members of the family. That came out to about $6 per person—in addition to any money they may have made shoveling snow or babysitting—so their choices have to be well-thought-out, rather than impulsive, even if I do admit that many of my presents for people are truly impulsive. We worked secretly wrapping each gift, attaching bows, and trying to keep the contents of the package un-guess-able. It's a happy time when we think of others instead of ourselves. (Except for the wish list taped to the refrigerator.)

By the 24th of December, our tree was up and decorated, as were many other spots in our house. The stockings were hung by the chimney with care, and we certainly hoped St. Nicholas would be there!

(read next story: Actions Speak Louder Than Words)

By 6 p.m. we had been to church, where we were treated to a lovely silent, music only, interpretation of the story of the birth of Jesus, as seen through the eyes of the children in the parish. No one seemed to mind the extra time the service took because it was so beautiful. It was a much-needed contrast to the season of hectic spending. Fr. Mike, as usual, charmed the children with his obvious enthusiasm and enjoyment while talking to them. We greeted him after the service and invited him to come for Christmas dinner, but he had other plans, so we invited him to come to Greg's birthday, which is just a couple days into the new year. As we left for home, I gave him an open invitation to drop in if he wanted to get into the craziness of our family during Greg's birthday.

Our family walked into the house to see that Santa had not arrived yet. Knowing that he had many houses to get to in just one night, our kids didn't panic. I'm sure they know of their parents' involvement in the life of Santa by now, but they still keep their younger childhood beliefs alive. We ate a small meal, had the kids put their gifts for each of us under the tree. Then, we, headed for bed, knowing morning would come very early. (Of course Greg and I had to sneak down the stairs again to put the kids' gifts under the tree and eat the cookies they had left on a plate for Santa.) I think Greg noticed there was no golf club sized box, *he probably figured I would sneak downstairs much later to place it where it would be easily seen.*

Christmas morning, we were up early. Well, at least the kids were up early. We could hear the whispers and giggles as they shook some of the gifts and tried to guess what was in each one. Even Bill was up early. The doorbell made Greg and I jump out of bed. There was Bill, standing in our living room, putting more packages by the tree. All of us were still in our pajamas, and we decided it would be more fun to open the gifts under the tree, then eat breakfast and get dressed. Since we went to church yesterday, we had a lot of time to enjoy everything more slowly without the mad dash to get to church.

I noticed that Greg was quieter than usual. He loves to see the kids break open their gifts, but today he expected to be the one getting a gift that would make him joyful, too. As we continued the madness, it was wonderful! Then Greg and I handed each kid a package so that they all opened one gift at the same time.

"A phone, I got a phone!" yelled Gracie.

"So did I," exclaimed Katie.

"I hope I did, too," said Kevin, as he tore into his gift. "Yay," he shouted and held the phone up in the air.

*We decided not to tell the kids about our rules for phone use until another time when they might be able to focus better.*

When the last gift was opened and we had all hugged and thanked each other, Bill and Greg offered to pick up all the wrapping paper and no longer needed boxes. Everyone else helped to get breakfast ready. While the food was good, I think we could have served the kids raw eggs and bacon with burnt toast, and they wouldn't have noticed. Their minds were somewhere else . . .

Adults seldom get toys for Christmas. They usually get helpful gadgets for the kitchen or garage workbench. So we are more likely to sit around talking to each other. Bill and I seemed to be holding up the conversation because Greg seemed a bit let down. I didn't know how to console him. I knew something he didn't know, but I didn't want to give away the secret. So, I let him feel a bit like any kid feels when he doesn't get the one gift he had hoped for.

We had an early dinner so that Bill could get home to await a phone call from a good friend on the East coast.

Only the three munchkins had jokes:

> Kevin: "Why did Santa Claus get a parking ticket on Christmas Eve?
> A: He left his sleigh in a snow parking zone." ***
>
> Katie: "Why are Christmas trees so bad at sewing? A: They always drop their needles." ***
>
> Gracie: "Who do dogs wait for on Christmas Eve? A: Santa Paws" ***

After Bill left, the kids were pretty excited about their phones, so we sat them down and told them, "We know you're excited about your phones. You already figured out how to charge them. Keep them charged, because you never know when you'll really need your phone for an emergency. If you ever see something bad, don't be afraid to call 9-1-1 and report what you see or hear," said their dad.

"We'll help you put four of your friends' phone numbers on your phone so you can call them easily. However, we're going to limit you to three 15-minute calls after school or after dinner. You may take your phone to school, but no calls to anyone but your dad or me. Basically, your phone is for emergencies or when you feel a need to talk to one of us, so keep it in your pocket or desk during the day. If Mr. Arnold confiscates it for misusing it, we will support his decision. At eight p.m. the phones go into the drawer in the dining room. Any questions?"

"No, Mom, we understand," said Gracie. The twins nodded their heads in agreement.

"This is the best gift—ever! Thanks, Mom and Dad!," they exclaimed. We were almost overwhelmed by their hugs and kisses.

Because the next day was a no-school day, we promised the kids they could use their phones to call their friends. Then they put their phones in the dining room drawer

I noticed that Greg sat for a long time just staring at the Christmas tree and all the opened gifts underneath it. I asked him if he was OK. He said, "Yes, it was a delight to see the kids so excited about their gifts, especially those phones." Then I heard him sigh and say to himself, *"Well, maybe* **'I Counted My Chickens Before They Were Hatched.'** *Still, my birthday is coming soon . . ."* Then he got up and went upstairs to bed. .

(. . . to be continued—go to Rule of Thumb)

***funnyeditor.com

# ACTIONS SPEAK LOUDER THAN WORDS

## Father Mike

It's the most wonderful time of the year . . . and for those who are actively involved at St. Brendan's Church, it is also the busiest time of the year. This year we are going to be treated to a surprise thought up by the younger kids in the religious education classes. Their teacher is Patty, the woman who helped us bring the Stewart kids into the Church last May. Her husband and some parents offered to help her.

Their plan was to have all the kids participate in a bumpy sidewalk procession of Joseph, Mary, and the Baby Jesus through our main street from the library to the church on Christmas Eve. They enlisted the help of several parents to find a suitable, sturdy wagon with sides that could accommodate two small children and a baby doll, sew costumes for all the children, make crooks for the shepherds, and offer to be helpers as the kids moved through the town. The smaller kids could be angels or shepherds, the older boys would be the three Kings or could pull the wagon through town. Two children were asked to be Joseph and Mary. The little girl was chosen because, besides being small, she had a new baby sister (with a baby wrapped in swaddling clothes, it doesn't matter who the baby is.) She would also be more comfortable carrying the real baby from the back of the church to the front, escorted by Joseph and a dozen angels. There was even a small manger set in front of Joseph and Mary's chairs. The shepherds and Kings would come through town, walking behind the wagon to the delight of all the spectators who may not be going to the church, but who would be thrilled to see kids they knew as they walked by.

For a few weeks, there was a lot of activity, and the

excitement began to build among the workers. The majority of our parishioners were not aware of the treat that awaited them. Patty did talk the kids through the whole ceremony, but she realized they would need to have a practice through the town and the procession into the church. She believed most things would go according to plan, and she also knew that adults are very forgiving of children who might forget what to do or need a little prompting.

Greg and Becky would be ushers, along with Andy and Rachel Davenport. Gracie, Kevin, Katie, Tristan, Cece, Mary, and several of their friends were in the children's choir. Everything was prepared. (Or at least we hoped it was.)

On Christmas Eve, the church was ready to receive the Holy Family. The kids' choir had one more short rehearsal, and the poinsettias were set around the altar. It was a nice day, not to cold or windy. At 4:00, the angels, shepherds, Joseph, Mary and the three Kings gathered at the library. The wagon was ready to receive its precious occupants. Two fifth grade boys were ready to pull the wagon. The angels would lead the procession through town, followed by the wagon carrying Joseph, Mary, and a doll wrapped in a blanket. Behind them would walk the shepherds, with the three Kings coming at the end. A fifth grade girl would lead the angels down the sidewalk to the church, while a few parents of the angels would stop traffic at the two crosswalks.

At 4:00 p.m. people began to arrive at the church. People are often annoyed to come to church on Christmas Eve and find someone else sitting in their pew. Being a smaller parish community, our church has the capacity to hold a larger group than normal, so everyone can find a seat— even if it isn't in their favored pew. I took my place at the front door of the church to await the procession. With me were the parents of little Gina, who would have the honor of being the real Baby Jesus. While we couldn't see the procession at first, we could hear the sounds of the spectators clapping as the children walked by.

Finally, they crossed the street and headed down toward the church. When the angels climbed the steps and got to the top step, Greg and I motioned for them to line up at the inner doors to the church. Then the boys pulling the wagon stopped to let Joseph and Mary get out and climb the steps. As they reached the front door, Patty motioned for the choir to begin singing one verse of O Little Town of Bethlehem. As the angels walked down the center aisle to stand behind the chairs waiting for Mary and Joseph, people began to stretch their necks to see the little cherubs. Then, Mary received her little sister Gina from her mom, and with Joseph, the three of them went down the center aisle to their chairs. They sat down facing the congregation just like a king and queen in front of their subjects. They didn't seem to be nervous at all.

The shepherds came in next and filled in the area in front of the angels and to each side of Joseph and Mary, as the choir sang one verse of The First Noel. Finally, the Three Kings processed in to one verse of We Three Kings. As they sat down, a hush came over the church. It was a magical moment as the adults saw and appreciated the simplicity of the Christmas story that the children acted out without saying a word. Baby Jesus, Mary and Joseph came to St. Brendan's that afternoon and reminded all of us that **'Actions Speak Louder Than Words.'**


(Return to Don't Count Your Chickens)

# A RULE OF THUMB

## Becky and the Kids

O ur kids are generally independent. They have different interests and activities. Very seldom do they come together, except at mealtimes. As **'A rule of thumb,'** Greg and I insist on a daily time, usually dinner, to share what's going on, what was fun, what made us angry or sad, and a chance to plan for the coming week. Occasionally, the kids will have a play date for lunch or a dinner with a friend's family.

We made it through Christmas, so now we're gearing up for Greg's birthday. It's just a few days into the New Year, so in some ways it's pretty low-key compared to the rush of the holidays. The kids still had some vacation time left, so I figured they would want to be with their friends, playing with the inevitable pile of new toys each of them would have received from Santa or as a Hanukkah gift.

I know that my husband will eat just about anything, but his favorite meal is baked chicken, mashed potatoes, gravy and veggies. Of course his birthday cake would be chocolate. It seemed to be popular with everyone, including Uncle Bill, Fr. Mike and our two grown kids, Beth and Nate. Since his birthday wasn't near a Friday, calling it a Fabulous Friday dinner wasn't possible, so we called it a Terrific Tuesday meal.

The chicken was in the oven for over an hour when Katie appeared in the kitchen. "What are you doing, Mom?" she asked, even though she could see what I was doing.

"I'm starting dinner. Tonight will be special, remember? It's your dad's birthday celebration. Do you kids have your gifts for him wrapped?" (I didn't know what they had gotten him; it would be a surprise for me, too.)

"Yes, our gifts are wrapped. What are you making? Can I help? Mary has gone to visit her grandparents today, so I'm all alone."

"Since your dad loves chocolate cake, why don't you get out the package of cake mix and follow the directions? First, you have to preheat the oven. Look for the temperature on the box."

Amazingly, Kevin and Gracie appeared in the dining room together.

"Hey, Mom, we don't have anything to do. We're bored. What could we do?"

"Come into the kitchen and help Katie and me make your dad's birthday dinner. Please wash your hands."

"Here's what we're going to do. Gracie, you get the potatoes out of the pantry."

"How many potatoes do I use?" Gracie asked, eager to help but unsure of what to do. I told her, "'**A Rule of Thumb'** is to make 1/2 pound of potatoes per person. You can use our kitchen scale to weigh them. How many pounds do you need for 9 people?" Gracie thought, *Kevin should be doing this. He's the one who loves math.*

"I think I need 4.5 to 5 pounds of potatoes."

"Go for it, Gracie. Kevin, your job is to cut the potatoes into equal-sized smaller pieces after they're peeled and to place them in the pan with water that just covers them. Add one teaspoon of salt. We can always add more when we eat, but it's hard to remove the salty taste once the potatoes are cooked. Turn on the burner to heat up the water."

"This is fun, Mom," he said, as he began to cut the peeled potatoes on a cutting board.

Then I turned my sights to Katie. "How are you doing with the cake mix, honey? Do you have all the additional stuff like the eggs, water, and the oil ready to stir into the cake mix?"

"I'm doing it pretty well, Mom. What cake pan should I use?"

"Do you want to make a round cake, or a rectangular cake?"

"I think a rectangular cake would be the easier one to cut."

"Good choice. Mix all the ingredients together and pour the batter into this rectangular pan. I'll grease the pan for you so that the cake won't stick when we cut it. Be careful putting it into the oven."

We were like a well-oiled machine—working so smoothly together. The cake and the chicken were in the oven, so while we waited, Gracie got out the plates and glassware and set the table. Katie helped with the silverware and napkins. Kevin went downstairs to get three extra chairs for Nate, Beth, and Fr. Mike. Gracie got the balloons I had hidden down there. I knew the chicken would take longer than the cake, so after about 30 minutes, I asked, "Katie, is the cake ready to take out of the oven?"

"How can I tell if it's done? What should I do?"

"Take the cake out of the oven. A good **'rule of thumb'** is to stick a toothpick into several spots on the cake. If the toothpick comes out clean, the cake is done. If there is sticky chocolate on the toothpick, then the cake needs to bake a little longer."

"I stuck it four times. The toothpick is clean, so I think it's done baking," said Katie, confidently, "but Mom, what does **'a rule of thumb'** mean?'"

"**'A rule of thumb'** is a guide based on people's practical experience, rather than some law. Many people have come to believe that inserting a toothpick and having it come out clean means the cake is done. There is a suggestion of baking time on the box, but sometimes that isn't accurate. Kevin, please tape the balloons to the chairs. Gracie, you can drain and mash the potatoes. We'll add a little milk and butter as you mash them." I took the chicken out of the oven to let it sit for a few minutes before carving it. I put the gravy and veggies into the microwave to get them hot.

There was a knock at the front door. Fr. Mike and Uncle Bill walked in and greeted all of us warmly. Both of them commented on the great smells coming from the kitchen. They had just taken off their coats when the sound of a car in the driveway told us that Beth and Nate had arrived. Nate announced that he saw Greg's car coming down the street. We all moved into a semi-circle around the table in the dining room. When Greg walked in, we greeted him loudly, "Happy Birthday, Dad;" "Happy Birthday, Greg." "Happy Birthday, honey!"

We all took a turn hugging him and congratulating him on making it through another year. Then as Greg, Bill, Beth, Nate, and Fr. Mike sat down, the rest of us hurried to the kitchen. Kevin put the mashed potatoes into two bowls. Gracie put the veggies into two dishes, I put the gravy into two small pitchers, and Katie brought out a large pitcher of cold water. When all the food was on the table, Fr. Mike said a short blessing over the food and prayed for all of us, especially his good friend, Greg, the birthday boy. Then we dove into the food; it always strikes me as a very special ritual to pass the food to each person at the table. Smiles abound and everyone is very polite. Soon after beginning to eat, Greg said, "Hey, it's my birthday dinner. Where are the jokes? It isn't a real party without them. OK, I'll start while you all think."

Greg: "What did the cows say on New Year's Eve? A: Happy Moo Year!" ***

Kevin: "What do you get when you cross a dog with a calculator? A: A friend you can count on." ***

Mom: "Why does Mrs. Claus love Christmas Eve? A: It gets her husband out of the house." ***

"Hey", said Greg. "Is that the way you really feel about me?"

"Of course not, sweetie," said Becky as she winked at Bill.

137

Bill:  Why do people wear shamrocks on St. Patrick's Day?
A:  Because real rocks are too heavy." ***

Gracie: "What kind of car does Mickey Mouse's wife drive? A:  A Minne Van" ***

Mike: "Where does the pepperoni go on vacation?
A: To Italy, to the Leaning Tower of Pizza" ***

Katie:  What did the pizza say to the gorgeous topping?
A:  I never SAUsage a beautiful face!"  ***

Beth:  "What animal makes the best lock smith? A:  A Mon-key" ***

Nate: "What is a zoo vet's biggest problem?
A:  A giraffe with a sore throat." ***

Of course, there was a period of laughter and giggles. When we were done eating, we had some time while we cleared the dishes for Katie and I to prepare the cake with some candles (eight, each representing 6 years of his life.) We lit the candles and Katie carried it to the table and set it in front of her dad. We sang *Happy Birthday*, and he blew out the candles. We clapped and immediately set our sights on the cake. It looked yummy.

"Who wants cake?" The question was rhetorical, I didn't need any answers, but I asked it anyways. I cut a piece for everyone and added a scoop of ice cream. We ate dessert before the gift-giving began. There was a small table in the dining room that had several small gifts on it. One by one the kids brought over a gift. I knew Greg was hoping, maybe even expecting golf clubs, but he could see that the wrapped gifts were too small to be clubs.

Gracie gave him a cushion for his chair at work, which was wooden and quite hard. "Thanks, Gracie, you knew I really need this. I'll think of you every time I sit down." We all laughed.

Katie handed him a package that contained a new wallet, with a special place to put his badge so it could be easily seen when he needed to show it to someone quickly.

Kevin gave him new tennis socks to replace some worn-out ones.

I gave him a bottle of his favorite aftershave.

Nate and Beth went together to get him a subscription to National Geographic.

Bill offered to take the kids one day when Greg wanted to get away (with or without me.)

While he was very gracious and grateful for all the gifts he had received, I could tell he was really disappointed at not getting any golf equipment. He realized he had **'counted his chickens before they were hatched.'**

Beth and Nate excused themselves. They needed to get home, since they lived about 45 minutes from our house. Nate and Beth had come together. Their spouses stayed home because both their babies had colds. Just when everyone else was getting ready to go home, there was a knock on the door and Maddie and Mitch Lanoski walked in. They are very good friends of ours, and our kids' self-chosen grandparents.

"Gee, we're sorry we got here so late. There was a big accident on the highway, and we had to go way out of our way on the detour.

"We would have called, but someone forgot to charge our cell phone," said Maddie, looking directly at Mitch. Maddie and Mitch sat down in the empty chairs.

"Would you like something to eat, a piece of birthday cake, maybe?"

"We did get a bite to eat before we got here, but a piece of cake would be great," said Maddie.

"Oh, my gosh," said Mitch. "I completely forgot it was

your birthday, Greg. I think we've been driving all day with your birthday present in our trunk. Wait while I go get it."

I saw a glimmer of hope in my husband's eyes as Mitch left and then returned with a long, slim gift.

"I think this belongs to you. Happy Birthday," said Mitch as he handed the wrapped gift to Greg. Then he winked at me and smiled.

It was like Christmas morning all over again. Greg tore into the paper and exclaimed with a cry of joy, "Golf clubs, I got golf clubs."

Then the kids brought out a few other little gifts for their dad: golf balls, a towel, a water bottle, and tees. Bill and I decided he might want to pick out his own golf bag and additional clubs. That could wait until he decided if he liked playing golf or not.

That night, as we got into bed, Greg turned to me and said, "I was so sure you would get me those clubs because they were on my refrigerator Christmas list. But Christmas came and went and my birthday was almost over—still no clubs. It was agonizing because I was *so sure* you would get me the one thing I wanted so much. You taught me a valuable lesson. I realized that it should be **'a rule of thumb'** not to **'count your chickens before they're hatched.'** Just one more reason why I love you *more* than my new golf clubs!"

***funnyeditor.com

# GET THE HANG OF IT

## Kevin

February is the best month of the year—next to December—because it's our birthday month. Katie and I look forward to our birthday almost as much as Christmas. Sure, there are less presents, but Mom makes the day really special by inviting Uncle Bill, Fr. Mike, our special grandparents, Mitch and Maddie, and our new relative, Uncle Tim.

So far, our grandparents have said they can't come because Grandma Maddie is ill. Uncle Tim said he would fly in the day before our birthday and stay for a few days after it. We were really excited to know that he was coming.

Another thing that makes our day so much fun is that Mom makes our favorite meal: "OK, what will it be this year? Any change from the last two years? Are you still in love with mac and cheese, chicken fingers, and a chocolate cake with mint chocolate frosting and a yellow cake with strawberries on top?"

"Wow, Mom—hooray!" Katie cheered. "You did it again. You have a great memory. That's what I'd like."

"Now how about you, Kevin? What would you like to eat?"

"Same for me, Mom. Yum, yum, I'm getting hungry already."

"Well, save your hunger for later. Tonight we're having liver and onions. You'll love it."

"Oh no," cried the twins, "You wouldn't do that to us, would you?"

"OK, OK, I'll think of something else," promised Mom. (She didn't go with us to the airport, so that gave her time to think of a *real* dinner!)

When Uncle Tim arrived, we met him at the airport and

chatted and giggled nonstop all the way home. We were a little tired from the ride and Uncle Tim was exhausted from his long day traveling, so we had a quiet supper—no liver and onions, no jokes, just small talk about things that had happened to us since the last time we saw him.

After dinner, Kevin thought: *"I like having visitors, especially overnight visitors, because I get to sleep on the downstairs couch. If I'm very careful and keep the volume very low, I can watch TV in the dark as long as I can before I fall asleep. I put the timer on so the TV isn't on all night."*

Katie and I were up early today. We only have about 13 hours to celebrate, so we wanted to get going early. When we came downstairs, Mom, Dad, and Uncle Tim were already eating breakfast and drinking coffee. I tried coffee once—yuck! They were happy to see us and reacted by shouting "Happy birthday, Kevin, Katie." Then we got our breakfast cereal and a few bowls because we knew Gracie would be joining us soon.

Friday is the best day of the week, the last day of classes. Time seemed to crawl all day, even though we took part in a fascinating experiment by a visiting scientist from the Research Park. He showed us a short film about something called a Van de Graaff Generator and showed us how electrons repel or are attracted to each other. We jumped when he showed us how to create a spark between two metal balls, and laughed when we saw how static electricity can cause a person's hair to stand straight out on his or her head. He gave us some tips about thunderstorms, and how to keep ourselves safe when a storm comes up.

Mom had made some cookies for us to share with our classmates before the bell rang. Everyone sang and said "Happy Birthday" to us.

When we got home, Uncle Tim said he had a surprise for us, but we needed to have our homework done before he would tell us what it was. Even Gracie had to do her homework. Of course we complained, but we did sit down at the kitchen table and work on several assignments. When the three of us were finished, Uncle Tim said he would reveal his secret after dinner when we opened our gifts. We pleaded with him to tell us, but he refused. So we just had to be patient and wait. That was harder than doing our homework.

Katie and I were sent on an errand to the Ice Cream Emporium to buy our favorite ice cream. It only took about 30 minutes, but by the time we returned to the house, Gracie, Uncle Tim and Uncle Bill had decorated the dining room with balloons, set the table with colorful napkins, and put out little hats for each of us to wear. We even had little party horns. Uncle Tim was about to see the real Stewart family in action. Mom and Dad had worked together furiously to prepare the food. Each cake was ready with candles for either Katie or me.

When dinner conversation took a little lull, we kids started in with the jokes:

> Kevin: "Did you hear about the guy who got hit in the head with a can of soda?
> A: He was lucky it was a soft drink!" ***

> Gracie: "Why do grizzlies make good baseball players?
> A: They can catch bear-handed." ***

> Katie: "Why did the echo get detention?
> A: She kept talking back to the teacher." ***

Soon our other family members joined in the fun:

> Uncle Tim: "How do football players deal with their problems?
> A: They tackle them head-on." ***

> Mom: "Why shouldn't you buy things with velcro?
> A: They're a total rip-off!" ***

Uncle Bill: "Why did the dog get
embarrassed?
We all shouted the answer: A: Because
he was  barking up the wrong tree" ***

We laughed because we remembered that Kevin was accused of barking up the wrong tree  tree when he blamed Katie for taking his new comic book.)

Dad: "How do you know the sun will rise
again? A: It will dawn on you." ***

Fr. Mike: "What kind of motor vehicle is
in the Bible? A: Honda, because the apostles
were all in one accord."  ***

After we had finished eating, Katie and I listened to everyone sing *Happy Birthday* to us. We blew out the candles on each of our cakes and enjoyed our favorite-flavored cakes and ice cream. Then it was time to open our gifts. Mom and Dad gave us new boots to wear in the snow. Gracie gave us new mittens and warm knitted hats made by one of our neighbors. Fr. Mike promised to give each of us a donut of our choice on Sundays for one month. *Of course we had to behave all week in order to deserve his treat.* Uncle Bill and Uncle Tim looked at each other and made a drumroll on the table. When we were silent and looking at them, they made their announcement:

"Uncle Bill and I would like to take the two of you downhill skiing this weekend at a resort up in the foothills. The downhill runs aren't that steep, so we think you'll **'Get the Hang of It'** quickly. If you would like to come, Gracie, we would love to have you join us."

"Would that be OK with the two of you?" asked Gracie, hesitating to come when it wasn't her birthday.

"Of course we want you to come—we're the Three Munchkin Musketeers, remember? None of us has ever gone downhill skiing. It will be fun to do it together."

"OK, then 'yes,' Uncle Tim, I would love to come along."

"Oh dear," said Dad, seeming to be sad. "That will leave your Mom and me home all alone all weekend. What will we do with our free time?" Dad looked at Mom and winked. *I don't think they would have minded if we had left tonight,* thought Uncle Bill.

The next day, we kids were so excited we could hardly sit still to eat breakfast. Mom made a list of things we needed to take in our backpacks. All of us would rent our equipment at the resort. By 9:30 a.m. we were ready to pack ourselves into the car. It was a beautiful day and the weekend promised to treat us to nice weather. It was a two-hour drive to the resort, which was nestled in some rolling foothills. The ski runs could be seen from the highway. Our nervousness grew a little as we got closer to the time that we had to put on heavy, monster-like boots, a gigantic helmet, attach two long, curved wooden slats to our boots and slide down a hill with only two poles to help balance us. Nevertheless, we got out of the car and grabbed our gear.

The receptionist welcomed us and told us how to find our rooms. Both Uncles Bill and Tim were given keycards to get us into our rooms, which were connected. Katie and I have our own room while the three men (2.5 men?) would sleep in the other room. Katie suggested that we should leave the adjoining door open all night in case someone (Katie) got scared.

After we finished the lunches Mom had packed, it was time to hit the slopes. Our uncles were incredibly patient with the three of us. We were happy to hear that we were going to have a lesson with a ski instructor to get us started. The three of us stood in front of her—both excited and terrified. She told us, "My name is Mindy." "Our names are Katie, Kevin, and I'm Gracie." She smiled a lot and showed us how to stop by doing something she called a snowplow with our skis. Then we rode the smallest ski lift halfway up the hill. It was all we could do to keep from sliding away from Mindy as we got off the chairlift. She encouraged us to start down the hill and snowplow if we got going too fast. Katie stayed with Mindy, who talked her down the hill.

Gracie and I got to the bottom with only one fall each. It was a challenge to get up, but once we got our skis horizontal on the slope below us, it was easier to stand. Once all three of us were down at the bottom of the hill, Mindy said she would go up the hill with us one more time and would take us up a little higher on the slope. That meant we would go faster and have to work a little harder.

I took off confidently, with Gracie right behind me. We were confident enough to rely on snowplowing to keep us slowed down. Katie looked a little scared, but she started smiling half way down the hill. When we were all at the bottom, we said "goodbye" to Mindy. Now we were on our own. Uncle Bill suddenly showed up and asked how the lesson was.

"It was great," I said, "I'm ready to go again."

"How about you, Gracie?"

"I loved it, I'm ready to go again, too," she exclaimed.

"And you, Katie, how are you feeling?"

"I think I would like to stay on the bunny hill for a while to practice stopping. But tomorrow, I'll be ready to join all of you."

"I'll hang around with Katie now to make sure she develops her confidence. It won't take long for all of you to **'Get The Hang Of It'**—skiing! I'd say Day One was a huge success. Tomorrow will be even more fun."

Uncle Tim took a few runs on a steeper hill before he came down and relieved Uncle Bill, so he could test his expertise on a nearby more challenging slope. Both men seemed to be having fun, even when they were helping the three of us to develop our skills and increase our enjoyment. It was so much fun! When we left the ski area, we were really tired and very proud of our accomplishments. Like Uncle Bill said, "Tomorrow will be even more fun!"

We had a wonderful early dinner in the dining room.

Afterwards we took a short walk around the chalet (lodge). Later, we sat watching TV in Gracie and Katie's room, while our uncles called home to report in. At that point we didn't miss our parents enough to want leave the TV to talk to them. I heard Uncle Bill laughing. I figured he had just told our mom how all three of us ordered mac and cheese and hot dogs for dinner. Finally both our uncles came and said, "good night" and kissed us. Uncle Bill said, "The lifts don't start running until 9 a.m. tomorrow, so we don't have to get up too early. Sleep tight—and don't let the bedbugs bite!" We turned off the TV, left the door open into the other room and fell asleep quickly.

When we woke up and got dressed, we were surprised to see how sore some of our muscles were. Guess if you don't use them often, they let you know that they're there. We moaned and groaned a bit, but after a great breakfast at the resort dining room, we were eager to get started. Today we wouldn't have to spend time guessing our boot size and ski length. The people who hand out the equipment are very helpful and considerate. It wasn't long before we were in a lift line. It had snowed a few inches overnight, but now the sky was clear, so it was definitely a blue bird day.

As we rode the lift, we would gently swing our skis while we looked around at the beautiful, snow-covered hills. Our uncles went with us for the first run.

"After watching you, we think we can trust you on a slightly more challenging slope than the ever-popular 'bunny hill.' Be careful, watch out for other skiers,  keep together as much as possible and remember it's a 'pizza slice' to slow down and a 'French fry' to go straight.' If a problem develops, You have your cell phones and have your uncle Bill's number"

*I guess I can only speak for myself*, thought Kevin, *but I'm having a blast today!* (The reference to a pizza slice and a French fry contributed to his enjoyment!)

From the look on Gracie's face, I could tell she was having a great time, too. She and Katie had met a friend from school who spent some time with them. Katie seemed to relax more and ended each run with a smile and a sigh of relief. Eventually, she **'got the hang of it.'**

When it was time to leave, we kids begged to be able to stay just a little longer. Bill and Tim looked at each other and decided 15 minutes more would be OK. So we tried to make the most of the last bit of time we had.      Finally, we headed to the rental shop and turned in our equipment. Walking again in regular shoes was a really strange experience. We went back to our rooms and changed into our normal clothes. Our hair was a disheveled mess from the helmets, so we needed to spend some time brushing our hair. When we looked totally ready to be seen in public, we headed to the dining room for our last meal at the resort. This time Uncle Tim said, "You need to order something other than mac and cheese and hot dogs. Try a new food that matches your new experiences this weekend."

I decided, "I'd like mashed potatoes and chicken fingers. The potatoes will remind me of snow and the fingers will be the ski runs."

Gracie and Katie seemed to like that idea, so they wanted the same food. Uncle Tim shook his head—*there are so many other choices!* It felt sad to be leaving a place where we had so much fun, but now we were eager to see our mom and dad and tell them about our audaciously bold weekend. It was our best birthday gift—ever, although we may have said the same thing last year, and the year before!

When we got home, we grabbed our gear out of Uncle Tim's car and unceremoniously dropped it on the floor in the living room.

"Wait a minute," Mom groaned, "even though I am very glad to see the five of you, I'm going to need some help with all the laundry."

"It's not that bad, Becky," said Tim. "We wore the same clothes all weekend. Should only be one load. I'll give you a hand."

Since Uncle Tim planned to leave the following morning, we had a few more hours of fun with him. Instead of being a quiet meal like the one we had when he arrived, this one was full of lots of laughs.

Kevin: "Why couldn't a guy with glasses see very well? A: He didn't have jed-eyes." ***

Katie: "How did one orca ask the other one to be his Valentine? A: Whale you be mine?" ***

Gracie: "Why don't ostriches fly? A: Plane fares are so expensive." ***

Uncle Bill: "Why do horses make such good debt collectors? A: They can always get people to pony up." ***

"Hey, wait a minute," Kevin interrupted, "What does 'pony up' mean?"

"It means to pay all your debts right away," explained Uncle Bill.

Mom: "What did the pear say to the celery stick" A: Quit stalking me." ***

Dad: "What are you studying in math? A: Everything under the sum." ***

Uncle Tim: "What do you call an old snow man? A: Water!" **

Everyone seemed to like that one, so we ended our meal with a lot of giggles and a feeling that the best place to be was with family. After we cleaned the kitchen and dining room and folded the load of laundry in the dryer, we munchkins got ready for bed. Before we went upstairs, we thanked each of our uncles and hugged them until they cried that they were being squished. Mom and Dad told Uncle Tim that he would always be welcome here. In response to that, he said,

"As soon as I have a new set of jokes, I'll be back—and ready!"

As I went to bed, I asked myself: *"What did the rocket say to the astronaut? A: \*\*Have a blast!"* \*\*\*

We certainly did.


\*\*\*funnyeditor.com

# THE END DOESN'T ALWAYS
# JUSTIFY THE MEANS

## Kevin and Father Mike

In our town there's a big community center open to the public for lots of events. I've done some volunteer work at the program for people with disabilities to help them live full lives, even if they have some physical challenges. There are a few smaller rooms that can be used as meeting spaces, and a very large room that holds several hundred people, like for a wedding reception, a business conference or sales exhibits. That's what interested me most today. A huge comic book fair with sales of newer comics as well as collector items was going on this week. I couldn't wait to go. Comic books are my passion. Of course, not having enough money is my curse.

I wanted to stop there after school today, but my mom and dad have a thing about doing homework right after school, and they don't want me to go out on a school night. They said I could check out all the exhibits on Saturday morning, but by that time everything would be picked over and sold to those who came earlier in the week. I had to come up with a foolproof plan, one that would accomplish my goal of seeing the comics today. Surprisingly, I didn't care about missing supper because I could go forever without eating when comic books are involved. But I had to find a way to get them to say: "Yes" to my sure-fire plan to avoid coming home to do homework.

My plan took shape as I walked past the community center after school. I wanted to run inside just for a minute, but I knew that once I got inside the building, I wouldn't want to leave. That's when I saw Fr. Mike, the pastor at St. Brendan's, coming out of the center. He had a small bag in his hand—

most likely containing a few comic books. My family knows how much he likes to get comic books for his nieces and nephews (although he reads them first.) I thought: *If I told Mom and Dad he was there, I'm sure they would say that I could stay with him.* So, I called Mom and Dad, told them that I was with Fr. Mike, and would it be OK to stay with him as long as I got home by 7:00 pm? It was sneaky, but I was willing to put my life on the line in order to get first dibs on those comic books. My parents didn't even think twice about granting my request.

I spent lots of time walking around, seeing what was available for sale, and greeting some of my friends who were there with their parents. I managed to get Peter's dad to buy me a hot dog with mustard, catsup and pickle relish. At 6:45 pm I walked home by myself with two comic books in my own small bag. Gracie and Katie would have to wait to read them until I had finished them.

I walked into our living room right on time, and saw Mom and Dad still at the dining room table. The supper dishes had been cleared away, and they were enjoying a cup of coffee. I walked up to them and opened my bag to show them the comic books I had chosen. They asked me, "Did you have a good time with Fr. Mike?" I was just going to say, "Yes, we had lots of fun," when *he* came walking out of the kitchen, coffee cup in hand. My whole life passed in front of my eyes as I stared at him. I could only mumble, "Hi, Fr. Mike. What are *you* doing here?"

I looked at my parents and saw a tiny smile begin to form on their lips. Clearly, they were enjoying my discomfort.

"Fr. Mike stopped here earlier to ask if I could work for him tomorrow. We invited him to eat with us," said Mom.

"Hi, Kevin, good to see you. Did you enjoy the comic book fair? I was there earlier this afternoon, but I didn't see you. Oh, and by the way, did you know I have a superpower? It seems that I can bi-locate. That means I can be in two places at the same time. I never knew that before today. It's a miracle."

"Why don't you sit down and have some supper? Or did

you get something at the community center?" asked Dad.

"I ate, and I'm not very hungry right now," I admitted. I wanted to sink into the floor and become invisible, but no such luck. After a short time, Fr. Mike put down his coffee cup, said he had to leave, and walked to the door. After he said "goodbye" to my parents, he looked at me and asked, "Hey, pal, got a few minutes?" He looked at my parents for their approval. They nodded and motioned for me to follow Fr. Mike outside.

When we got onto the porch he said, "We need to talk. Your choice—swing or steps?" I sat down on the top step, and Fr. Mike sat one step lower. "I think we have a couple problems here tonight. One, you lied to your parents, and two, you involved me in your attempt to avoid their rules. You did an 'end run' by using me to get past your parents' rules in order to get what you wanted. It's a good football strategy, but not a very good way to treat the people who care about you." Then he looked at me and asked, "Would you say we're good friends?" When I said, "Yes," he continued: "Good friends need to trust each other. Do you think I might wonder if I can trust you now? Do you think your parents are going to be willing to trust you after what you did this afternoon?"

I wanted to cry. Of course, I wanted my parents and Fr. Mike to trust me. Now I was afraid I'd done a very bad thing, although it seemed harmless enough earlier today—clever, even.

"I want you and my parents to trust me. What I did was wrong. Please say you'll trust me again."

"I will trust you, kiddo, now and in the future, but you need to remember that **'The End Doesn't Aways Justify the Means.'** Even if you were successful in getting what you wanted —the comic books, something usually suffers: friendship, trust, respect—if you try to achieve your goal in the wrong way. I know you can do better, and I believe that you will. Friends who trust each other?"

"Friends who trust each other, I promise." We fist bumped. "Good night, Fr. Mike, and thanks!"

Now, I knew I had to face my parents. I would share with

them what Fr. Mike and I had talked about and I would promise them, too, that I would try very hard to be someone they could trust.  They confiscated my two comic books until Saturday night, so I never did get to read them early. Even Katie and Gracie read them before I did. I told myself: *From now on I'll save my 'end runs' for the football field.* But, hey, I'm only 11, so there are no guarantees!

# WE'VE GOT BIGGER FISH TO FRY

## Greg

As a detective, I try not to bring my work home. It's true that I do work at home, but that's mostly filling out reports, responding to requests from other police departments about information we, in Rainbow Falls or Riverview, might have regarding a particular case they are working on, and making phone calls. What I try to do is keep my emotions from spilling over in this high-pressure job and affecting my family. Today I was busy with four bank robberies that had happened over the past two weeks in our district. The robberies followed the same pattern, which suggested they were committed by the same people or at least had the same leaders. We spent the past several days interviewing witnesses at all four bank sites, working with evidence collectors, and doing countless searches on the internet.

When I got home today, I was exhausted. I was worried that I might snap at my wife or the kids when I felt so stressed. So, I decided to go on a bike ride to let off a little steam (get rid of some stress and excess energy) and to forget a little about the day's problems.

"Hi, sweetie," I said to my wife, Becky, when I kissed her and gave her a hug. "Where are the kids?"

"They're in the backyard playing croquet. Do you want to join them? They're always looking for an adult to beat. It's your turn."

"Sorry, honey, today was very unpleasant. I'm not in the mood to have fun . . ."

"Since when is getting embarrassed by your kids at a backyard game fun?" I put my arms around him and said,

"Rough day, huh?"

"Like sandpaper on my brain," I said. "I'm going to take a shower. That should help a lot."

"Go for a bike ride first, and then wash your worries down the drain, honey, you'll feel better."

Showers are wonderful things. So are the smells that come from the kitchen before a great meal. Tonight the smells were especially tantalizing—my favorite comfort food—baked chicken with mashed potatoes, gravy, veggies, and chocolate cake for dessert! I was beginning to feel grateful for my life and family. The kids didn't let me down. They came prepared with jokes especially for me:

Katie: "What do you call a cat that's in trouble with the police? A: A purr-petrator" ***

Gracie: "What do you call a flying police officer? A: A Helicopper." ***

Kevin: "What did Dad say when he was asked to say Grace? A: Grace" ***

"Thanks for helping me forget today with those jokes. All of you have taken me away from my frustration and made me feel better."

"Why are you frustrated, Dad, is it anything we did?"

"No, of course not. The three of you are angels compared to the people I have to work with daily."

"Who made you so mad today? Can you tell us?" Gracie wanted to know how the three of them could be angels when compared with the people at her dad's work.

"Well, I can't talk about specifics, but there are some bad people in our area that are making the police and the bankers very unhappy. We'd like to catch and arrest them, but that might not solve our problems."

"Why not, Dad, wouldn't that stop their crimes?" Kevin saw a clear connection between crimes and the criminals.

"No, Kevin, finding and arresting the people who are committing the crimes probably won't stop anything for long. We're convinced that the young people committing the crimes are working for other, more dangerous, folks. We want to catch the robbers, for sure, but, frankly, **'We Have Bigger Fish to Fry.'** We want to catch the leaders, too. Do you understand that?"

"Sure, Dad, you have a very difficult job. I hope you catch all these bad people." Gracie seemed really concerned, as did Kevin and Katie, if I read their faces correctly. Even Becky looked worried.

"It's OK," I tried to reassure them. "I may have a tough job, but coming home to all of you, even at your worst moments (and I looked at all three kids as I said that) is so much more enjoyable." I smiled at Becky and gave her a wink that told her even our little disagreements were minor.

*Yes, the world is full of people who want to do evil and drag us down, but there are many more people, known as family and friends, who rise above the rest and lift us up with their love.*

***funnyeditor.com

# CAUGHT BETWEEN A ROCK
# AND A HARD PLACE

## Becky, Gracie and Uncle Tim

Much to our surprise and delight, the kids' Uncle Tim called and said he had a few days off and would like to come visit us. The kids were very excited to see him again. He had made a great first impression on them when he met his nieces and nephew for the first time last October. Since then, he'd been here two more times. Immediately, they began to plan all of his time:

"It's Spring Break, we've got to think of neat things to do while he's here," said Gracie. "Let's put our heads together and come up with a plan, maybe even a schedule."

"Hold on, you can't have him all the time. He may have other things he would like to do, and your mom and I would like to spend some time with him, too." Greg was trying to rescue Uncle Tim from a very active few days. "I tell you what, you can plan daytime things for him, but your mom and I get him to ourselves in the evening—unless we decide to do something as a family like watch a movie or go out for pizza and hang out at the Emporium." The Rainbow Falls Ice Cream Emporium is really an awesome place that serves ice cream and a limited menu that appeal to everyone. There's also a popular jukebox that eats up lots of our quarters.

"That sounds like a good plan to me," said Gracie, "how about the two of you?" Kevin and Katie nodded their heads in agreement.

Having settled that much, they went off to do their own activities. Kevin likes going to the gym, Katie likes to read, and Gracie likes to go to the pet store to see if she can help out in any way.

When Uncle Tim arrived that night, all hands were on deck and ready for inspection. We were all delighted to see him, and the look on his face showed us that he felt the same way.

"Uncle Tim," yelled all three kids as they raced up to hug him. It took a while for him to be able to shake hands and hug Becky and me because he had three kids hanging on him. "We'resogladyou'rehere.Weplannedallkindsofthingstodo." The kids seemed to say all that in rapid unison. It caused him to put up his hands and declare, "Hey, hey, slow down, I can't understand what you're saying." The three munchkins looked at him, thinking *he* wasn't listening fast enough.

More slowly, they said, "We're so glad you're here. We planned all kinds of fun things to do."

"OK, OK, Let me get settled. I'm guessing I get Kevin's room so he can sleep on the couch downstairs. I know he loves the couch."

After about 30 minutes, Tim came downstairs to his fan club. All of us wanted to know how his flight was, how long could he stay, and was there anything he wanted to do in the big town of Rainbow Falls or Riverview?

"Actually, I would like to go up to Riverview, again. I'd like to see if I can find out any more information about my sisters during the years I was away from them."

"Again, Bill can help you with that," Greg reminded him. "He knew the kids two years before we did. He may think of other people to talk to."

By the time Tim was ready for bed, the kids had his daytime schedule all figured out. Luckily, he's a good sport about doing some things with kids that he had never done before: Kevin wanted him to go to the climbing wall at the gym, Gracie wanted him to go to the pet store with her to see all the animals, and Katie wanted him to go with her to the library to see a puppet show she and a few friends had worked up to entertain kids ages three to six.

"I'll be here Friday through Sunday. I'll leave early

on Monday morning. So we should have time to do all the things you have planned. I could spend some time during the afternoons with each of you. Saturday morning is a possibility, too."

"I get you Friday afternoon," said Kevin. "You and I will go rock climbing at the gym."

"I want you to come to my puppet show at the library on Saturday morning," said Katie. "You'll like it; it's a very funny story we wrote about a farmer who has trouble keeping his animals under control. They like to run away."

"We'll have fun on Saturday afternoon watching, petting, and walking the animals at the pet store," said Gracie. "I love holding the kittens and puppies the most."

"And, of course, you'll be our guest at our Fabulous Friday meal tomorrow, a fun event with dinner and a terrific dessert. I think we should invite Uncle Bill and Fr. Mike, too," Becky suggested.

"Great idea, honey. Tim, it will be a meal like no other."

All of us laughed—we know how crazy our meals can become.

On Friday morning, Bill took Tim up to Riverview to help him connect with some people who might have remembered his sisters. While he didn't find out much, he got a good picture in his mind of what they were like—two moms who were responsible young adults devoted to their kids.

In the afternoon, he and Kevin went to the gym and worked on the climbing wall. It was Tim's first experience, so he was slower and more careful than Kevin, who seemed like a speedy, tiny reptile by comparison. They worked out on the weight equipment and headed for home in time to take a shower before dinner.

Bill and Fr. Mike came to dinner that evening, and true to form, all of us came prepared to entertain the whole group:

Kevin: "How do basketball players eat chocolate

sandwich cookies? A: They dunk 'em." ***

Greg: "Why did the baseball player go to jail?
A: For stealing a base" ***

Becky: "What did the llama say it would bring
to the field trip? A: Alpaca lunch" ***

Bill: "What's the best way to get your kids'
attention?
A: Sit down and look comfortable." ***
   (Greg and I laughed the hardest.)

Gracie: "Why was the new feline mom always
so tired?
   A: She couldn't take catnaps any more." ***

Katie: "What time does Donald Duck wake up?
A: At the quack of dawn" ***

Tim: "Why were the teacher's eyes closed?
A: She couldn't control her pupils." ***

Fr. Mike: "What does a spy do when he gets
cold? A: He goes undercovers. ***


After the appropriate groans and laughter, we finished
eating. Tim told Kevin he was feeling the effect of wall climbing
on muscles he hadn't used for a long time. But he did say that he
had lots of fun. Kevin decided to take it easy on him and asked
him if he would play cards with him and the girls.

"Sorry, kiddo, but we get your Uncle Tim in the evenings,
remember? We want to spend some time with him, too," Mom
reminded us.

The kids were disappointed, but they found other things
to do to pass the time until they went to bed. We adults spent the

time listening to Tim repeat what he had told Bill about finding out only a little bit about his sisters, but it was better than nothing. Greg suggested that maybe the kids could spend some time tomorrow night talking about what they remembered about their moms. We had done that a year ago, and it seemed to help them keep the memory of their moms alive.

"I'd like that, if you think the kids will be OK with that. They're such a joy. What energy! I'm glad that tomorrow morning I just have to sit and watch Katie's puppet show at the library."

"How about a nice, quiet dinner tomorrow? We don't want to wear you out before you leave. It will take you a week to recover," Becky told him.

"Good night, I can't tell you how much I'm enjoying being here."

"The pleasure is ours," Greg assured him. He shook Tim's hand and wished him a good night's sleep. Tim kissed me on the cheek.

"See you tomorrow," he said.

The next morning Katie was up and eager to get going with her uncle Tim. "Are you ready for today?" she asked.

"Sure, honey, do I have time to eat breakfast with your mom and dad?" I'll be ready in 30 minutes."

Finally Katie said she needed to get to the library to get ready for her puppet show. When we got to the library, she pointed to my seat. As I sat there with about twenty other parents and their young ones, I felt a little sadness that I had never experienced the joys and trials of being a parent. The Stewarts were the closest thing to a healthy family I ever knew, and I wanted to be a part of it—forever. When the puppet show was over, Katie and I talked about it on the way out of the library.

"It was incredible, Katie. You and your friends did an amazing job. The puppet set was designed to be moved into different scenes; the puppet costumes and the voices of the different puppeteers were perfect. I'm so impressed that your little group wrote the script, designed the set, made the puppet costumes and put on a successful program. Good for you, honey." I put my arm around her shoulders and gave her a hug. Then the two of us headed for home.

"Who's turn is it to make lunch?" Mom asked when we were all together. The twins looked at each other with a smile on their faces.

"It's our turn, Uncle Tim. We hope you like mac and cheese."

"Sure do." (Like we said, he was a very good sport.)

As soon as lunch was over, Gracie grabbed her uncle's arm and told him it was time to go to the pet store.

"Are you ready? We need to get going." She literally dragged him through the front door.

"You know what I like about Rainbow Falls? It seems that you can walk everywhere. No need to have a car, is there?" observed her uncle Tim.

"Kevin, Katie and I like to ride our bikes, but Dad and Mom will give us a ride if we're late for school or the weather's bad."

When the two of us got to the pet store, I opened the door for her. When Gracie walked inside, she was greeted by several people, including a couple of staff members.

"This is my uncle Tim. He's visiting us for the weekend. He's going to help me walk the dogs and play with the kittens."

"Nice to meet you, sir. Gracie knows the routine around here, so we'll let her show you around. Make yourself at home," one of the staff members told him.

Gracie was so excited to get started. "First we'll walk the dogs. I can show you more of Rainbow Falls as we take the dogs out for some exercise. I usually walk two dogs at a time, but today I'm going to have you walk a dog named Grizzly. He's quite a handful. Wait until you meet him."

"A handful, huh? Are you sure I can handle him?" I was a little skeptical about my ability to walk a very eager dog. "I'll give you a few treats to give him. Then he'll love you," Gracie reassured me. "We won't have any trouble. The dogs know what to do."

Walking the dogs turned out to be fun and good exercise for the dogs and their leash holders. When we got back to the shelter, Gracie put the dogs into their correct cages and told me, "Now we get to play with the cats and kittens. I like taking them into a small room with some toys and a scratching post. We can give them a few pieces of food just to get them to come to us so we can pick them up. They're pretty independent."

After we played with the larger cats, we turned our attention to the kittens. As we sat there holding and petting them, Gracie began to act differently. She got very quiet and looked down at the kitten in her lap. She stroked the kitten, but she said nothing. It was such a strange change in her former excitement that I couldn't help but notice the difference.

"Are you OK, Gracie? Is anything wrong? You seemed to be having a good time, but now you're so quiet. What's going on, honey, do you want to talk about something?" I waited for her to answer. She continued to stroke the kitten on her lap. Her head was down, clearly choosing not to look at me.

"If I tell you something bad will you get mad at me or tell my mom?'

*As I've said before, I have very little experience with children, especially those having serious questions or problems. But this was no time for me to feel insecure.*

"Sure, Gracie, you can tell me anything and I won't get mad at you, but I may have to decide to tell your mom if what you tell me is serious."

She looked up at me, tears beginning to fill her eyes.

"I took $10 from my mom's purse to give to my friend, Lyra, so she can buy a special present for her mom's birthday."

"Where's the money now? Did you give it to Lyra?"

"No, I put it in the garage in my bike bag. I know Mom likes to look through our sock drawers if she thinks she might find missing things like money. What should I do, Uncle Tim?

I already told Lyra I have the money and will give it to her tomorrow at church. But if Mom sees that the $10 is gone from her purse, she's going to find out that I took it. She'll tell me to give it back. I can't let my friend down, but I can't get my mom angry, either. What should I do?"

"This is a problem we call **'Getting Caught Between a Rock and a Hard Place,'**" I said. "You have two choices, yet both of them are unpleasant. One, you could give the money back to your mom and apologize to her. That would let your friend down. Or, two, you could give the money to Lyra and let your mom be upset with you. Either choice will make someone unhappy with you. I can tell you what I think: I know enough about your parents to say your mom will want to know why you did it. Your loyalty to your friend may sway her feelings a bit, but she'll be upset that you didn't come to her first before going through her purse. That was disrespectful."

Gracie gave a big sigh and wiped her eyes. I could almost see the struggle going on inside her. 'I guess I should give the money back to my mom, but I really want Lyra to keep on being my best friend."

"You have to make the choice, Gracie. I can't do that for you. We probably should be heading home now."

That night the meal was quieter than the night before. *The food was so good that I wished Becky would come to live with me!*

When we were finished eating, Becky suggested that the kids share with me some of their memories of their mothers —my sisters.

Greg took down the big collage on the wall. "Do the three of you remember how we talked about your moms when we made this collage? You came up with some great memories. Why don't you tell your uncle about those things?"

After about an hour of their remembering things and sharing them with me, I felt a little overwhelmed with the feelings I now had about the two sisters I never really got to know as adults. I even shed a tear or two as I listened to the munchkins sharing their memories of their moms up until they were in the first grade. That's when their life with their moms stopped . . .

When the kids seemed tired, and I couldn't think of any more questions, the twins asked to be excused. Katie and Kevin went up to their rooms. Gracie, however, remained at the table. She began to twirl her hair. That was—a 'tell'—a sign that she had done something wrong, which made her mom look at her curiously.

"Mom, I have something to tell you," Gracie began. But Becky interrupted her and asked: "Is this about the $10 you took from my purse this morning?"

"How did you know about that?" Gracie looked at Tim with fire in her eyes. "You told her, didn't you? You told me it was my choice, but you told her first. I trusted you. Now I hate you!" Tim seemed a little overwhelmed by the force of Gracie's words. He watched her race up the stairs to her bedroom and slam the door.

I got up and walked to him, extending my hand, "Welcome to the *Hated Parents' Club*, Tim. You're really a member of our family now. Greg and I are old hands at dealing with this kind of behavior."

"Should I go up and talk with her? Will she even listen or talk to me?"

"I don't think you have to worry, Tim. Our kids have short memories when it comes to being angry with us. Wait a few minutes, then go up and have a chat with her."

Ten minutes later, I climbed the stairs to Gracie's room and gave the door a little tap. "Gracie, please, honey, may I come in?" I waited for a short time and heard nothing but a soft sniffling. Taking a chance, I opened the door. She was lying on her bed, all curled up as if she was protecting herself from a monster or a giant ape or maybe me.

"Gracie, sweetie, you and I need to talk. I don't want to us to spend a minute more with you having bad feelings about me. I'm sorry that you think you can't trust me anymore. That

166

makes me feel sad. Would you sit up so that we can talk?"

Gracie sat up, but didn't seem in a hurry to have a conversation. So I decided to keep talking, "Do you remember that we talked about being **'caught between a rock and a hard place'** this afternoon, how you had two choices to make and neither one of them was going to make you happy? I felt the same way when I saw your mom and realized that I had to choose between sharing with your mom what you told me or keeping your secret. I was **'caught between a rock and a hard place'** just like you. I made a decision to wait to see what you would do. I didn't know if she had already seen that the $10 bill was missing from her purse. I hoped that you would tell your mom tonight what you shared with me this afternoon. I didn't say anything to your mom. I'm very proud of you for being honest with your mom. I'm hoping you know how much I care about you and hope we'll still be friends. I don't want to go home Monday worrying that things are not good between us."

"We're OK, Uncle Tim. I'm sorry I said I hated you and couldn't trust you anymore. I think I understand how you felt when you didn't know how to choose. I guess respecting my Mom is more important than my friend Lyra's need for money for her mom's birthday gift.

"I know your mom will be more than willing to listen to you and help you with your friend's dilemma. I'll be happy to sit with you while you talk to your mom if you want me to."

The two of us walked downstairs to where Becky and Greg were sitting. Both of them put down the books they were reading.

Gracie reached into her pocket. "Here's your money, Mom."

Becky stood up and motioned for Gracie to sit on the couch (as I found out later, it was the place for a person or persons in trouble to sit) while she pulled the footstool close and sat on it with her knees touching Gracie's.

"Tell me what's going on. What do you need the money for?"

"I wanted to give it to Lyra so that she can buy her mom a

pretty gift for her birthday. I'm really sorry; I should have asked you to help me figure out a way to help Lyra get the money she needed. I told her I would give the money to her tomorrow at church. Now that I don't have the money, I'm afraid she won't want to be my best friend anymore. And you and Dad are probably upset with me. It's a mess. I don't know what to do."

"Does Lyra get an allowance? Did she want you to pay for the entire cost of the gift?" asked her mom.

"I don't know, she just said she needed $10."

"OK, tomorrow you and I will sit down with Lyra during the coffee hour and try to find a solution to her problem."

"Thanks, Mom. Did you hear that, Uncle Tim? You said she would help me."

"Wait a minute, honey, I'll help you tomorrow, but you owe me two nights in the kitchen helping me cook supper next week—cooking and doing the dishes. Agreed?"

"Agreed. Thanks again, Mom. I love you. I'm going upstairs. Goodnight Dad, good night Uncle Tim, I love both of you, too."

Gracie bounced up the stairs and was gone.

Greg looked at Becky. "So Uncle Tim was in on this? How about it Tim, did you tell her to confess tonight?"

"Nosiree (no-sir-ee), that was entirely her idea. I just listened and told her what I thought. I'm glad it worked out all right. What do you think you can do for Lyra and Gracie tomorrow? Do you think the three of you can come up with a solution to Lyra's problem?"

"Somehow everything seems better, happier, more creative when you have a doughnut in your hand," said Becky. "I'm going to bed now, too. Goodnight." She stooped to kiss her husband and Tim.

Greg looked at Tim. "It seems that one of our kids is always challenging our parenting skills. There's never a dull moment. Thanks for helping Gracie today. Our kids really have fallen in love with you."

"I can't believe I missed all this for so many years. I was

a fool for not looking for my family earlier. I feel like I made up some lost time tonight just by listening to the kids talk about their moms—my sisters."

"Our kids are surprisingly well-adjusted, considering all they've been through. Having you here is a very good thing for them. You're a connection to their moms."

The men said goodnight and headed for their rooms. When Greg walked into his bedroom, Becky was sitting on the bed, looking at some jewelry from a box on the top of her dresser.

"Hi, I was just looking at this jewelry I haven't worn for years. Perhaps something here will appeal to Lyra as a good gift for her mom. Sure would make things easier." She returned the box to the dresser and got into bed. "Goodnight, honey, I love you."

"Love you more", said Greg as he turned out the light.

Sunday morning, we were a little slow getting up, eating breakfast and getting ready for church. Even Uncle Tim seemed to want to sleep a little later.

"Gracie, would you come into my bedroom, please? Look at the pieces of jewelry I laid out on the bed. These are things I've had for many years, but haven't worn in a long time. Do you think any of these would appeal to Lyra? There are a few bracelets, a necklace, and a pair of matching earrings that go with this necklace."

"Oh, Mom, these are beautiful. I think I might like to have one of these bracelets if Lyra doesn't want it."

"Let's get one young girl taken care of, then you and Katie can take a look at what's left."

When we got to church, I saw Lyra, but didn't have the time to tell her that I didn't have the $10. She smiled at me and waved. I was a little nervous. I didn't know what I would do if she got mad at me or said she didn't want to be friends any longer. Church seemed to drag. I kept hoping it would be over, but Fr. Mike talked and talked and talked . . .

At last, we got to go downstairs for the coffee hour. I picked out my doughnut and a glass of orange juice and headed for the table where my mom was sitting with the rest of my family. "Mom, would it be OK to ask Lyra to come over here so we could talk to her?"

"Sure, honey, go get her."

"Everyone, Do you remember my good friend, Lyra? I think you know everyone here, except maybe my uncle Tim."

"Let's sit at that table for a little while," said my mom."

We moved over to another table, just the three of us, and sat so that Lyra's mom couldn't see or hear us, but we could see her if she got up to come toward us.

"Lyra, I couldn't give you the $10. I told my uncle Tim that I took it from my mom's purse. He convinced me to tell my mom. She was upset with me, but she wants to help you, don't you, Mom?"

"Sure I do, sweetie. Look at these pieces of jewelry, Lyra. They belong to me, but I would be willing to give you whatever you think your mom would like. Are you interested in a bracelet, a necklace, or earrings? There's even a ring here somewhere in this little bag." She spread out every piece of jewelry onto the table in front of Lyra. Her eyes got very big as she looked at the pretty items.

"Oh, Mrs. Stewart, I love this bracelet. It's exactly what I would like to give my mom. Do I need to pay you for it? I don't have any money. Gracie was supposed to get me that." (She looked at us and laughed.) "I'm sorry I got Gracie into trouble with you."

My mom handed Lyra the bracelet. She slipped it into her pocket as she walked back to her family. Mom looked at me and said, "Honey, I admire your sense of loyalty to your good friend, but next time, if you're asked to do something you know is wrong, don't let yourself get **'caught between a rock and a hard place.'**"

***funnyeditor.com

# ON THE SAME PAGE

## Greg and Kevin

Sixth grade is more fun than fifth grade, even though I loved Mrs. Quinn, our fifth grade teacher, who was my favorite teacher—ever! Mr. Arnold likes to give us projects to work on—sometimes we work with a group, sometimes we work alone. I will have to work on our newest project alone. The only help I can get is from Mrs. Davenport, the wife of our town's firefighter/ paramedic, Andy. She's the Mom of Tristan and CeCe, who volunteered to work with Mr. Arnold to help us with our questions about the project. Each of us has to interview someone we admire and tell why that person is so special to us. The idea is to give the class some knowledge about someone they may or may not know very well. We were encouraged to pick someone other than our family members because we already know them pretty well.

I've given this project a lot of thought. I want to get a good grade, and I want to think of someone no one else would choose. It took me about three days, when it just jumped into my head —Mr. McHugh! I have a strange relationship with Mr. McHugh. He owns the gym in town where our family has a membership. I've spent a lot of time and energy on the climbing wall, even got my uncle Tim to come climbing with me. Katie and Gracie come, as well as Mom, Dad, and Uncle Bill, but they like the pool, sauna, weight room and dance studio. He also owns the family business: three generations of family members working at the C.J. McHugh Gravel Company.

As I said before, I have a strange relationship with Mr. McHugh, one that no one else could claim, not even his kids:

When I was in foster care with my mom and dad three years ago, I pretended that climbing a great white tree was going to be my imaginary conquest of Everest. Problem was, the tree was in

172

the Gravel Company yard. I had to crawl under a fence with my loop of rope and begin my climb to a higher altitude. I used my rope to pull myself up the tree trunk and swing myself onto the first branch. I climbed to the top of the tree, branch by branch, and then I made a major mistake: I wasn't paying attention and stepped sideways, falling into the tree trunk. Long story, short, the fire department came, as well as Mr. McHugh, who gave the firefighters permission to cut down the tree that was planted years ago by his great-grandfather, but a tree that was obviously rotten now. He was genuinely kind and concerned about me. My family and I have been his friends ever since.

We were supposed to ask specific questions:

Me: "Mr. McHugh, where were you born? Did your ancestors come here from some other country? What kind of work did they do?"

Mr. McHugh: "I was born in Riverview a long time ago. However, my ancestors came to the US from Scotland way back in the 1800s. They lived in Pennsylvania for 15 years before moving west. They liked it here because there was a huge amount of rock and sand that could be broken down to make cement and concrete for construction."

Me: "My dad's family is from Scotland, too. How big is your family? Do some of your relatives work at the Gravel Company?"

Mr. McHugh: "Yes, Kevin, you've met most of my family. I have a wife, two sons and a daughter. For years, at least three people from the McHugh family have worked at the Gravel Company together. It truly is a family business."

Me: "You also are part-owner of the gym downtown. How is that different from your work at the Gravel Company?"

Mr. McHugh: (Laughing,) "Well the biggest thing is the lack of noise. The gym is much quieter. It's also more of a people job, which I like. It's fun to walk around and see people of all ages having fun and doing healthy things."

Me: "What's the biggest reason you've worked with rock, sand, cement and concrete all these years? Do you watch new building construction and think "'I helped supply some of these materials?'"

Mr. McHugh: "I love my job for that very reason. though I spend a lot of time in the office now, I still get to drive some of the heavy equipment, you know, things that smash rock and move big chunks of concrete and sand to other areas of our huge property. Say, Kevin, how would you like to sit in a few of our big machines, just to see what it feels like?"

Me: "Wow! Of course, I'd love to do that!" Soon he had me climbing up onto some of the biggest machines I have ever seen. I made me think that I might like to work for him. But I'd have to be older and bigger just to climb onto the driver's seat without someone pushing me up!

My report was almost finished when I had my last interview with Mr. McHugh. I asked him:

Me: "What would you have done with your life if your family hadn't built up this amazing business?"

Mr. McHugh: "Well, I never really gave it much thought because it was just expected that I would follow in my father's footsteps, but if I could have tried something else, I think I would have liked to be a park ranger. I like being outside, meeting people, and sharing with them my love of nature. However, my life has been great, so I wouldn't change a thing."

My dad arrived at the gym to give me a ride home. As I went into the front area to get my books and jacket, I heard Mr. McHugh say," That boy of yours is really something."

My dad agreed, but then he said, "Yes, and at the same time, he can be a real challenge to our otherwise dull life."

"I understand you there, Greg. Sometimes I wonder what it would be like if we'd never had our three kids. It sure would have been quieter and less stressful."

"Becky and I have those same conversations every once in a while, too. What would we be doing now if we didn't have kids?"

As soon as I heard that, I ran to the car. All of a sudden I was no longer interested in getting to know more about a man who thought his kids caused him stress, kids who were just bothersome. And my dad seemed to agree. Maybe he and Mom wished we weren't around. Maybe they wanted a quiet life, too. Now I didn't know what to think. I was confused. Dad came to the car. He unlocked it, and I got in the front seat. Once we were buckled in and on our way, Dad said, "How's your report coming along, Kevin? Is it finished? Mr. McHugh seems to have enjoyed working with you."

"I don't know, Dad, I don't think my report is that good. I think I want to choose someone else to interview."

Hearing me say that, my dad pulled over to the curb and stopped the car. He turned toward me, put his arm around my headrest and leaned close to me. "What's going on, kiddo? You've been working on this project for two weeks. You took pictures of the gym and big rigs. What happened? We were all taking pride in your work just a short time ago; it was fun for all of us to think that your time with Mr. McHugh has been valuable and informative. Now, you don't seem to be **'On the Same Page'** where we were before. Please, tell me what went wrong in the last 15 minutes."

"Do you really agree with Mr. McHugh that life would be less stressful and quieter if you didn't have me around? Do the girls and I cause trouble for you that makes you wish we would go away?" As I said that, my voice cracked and I could feel tears filling my eyes.

Dad reached into his pocket and handed me his handkerchief. "Kevin, listen to me very carefully. This is the second time that you've overheard part of a conversation and decided you knew and understood the whole thing. I want to get you back **'on the same page.'** Yes, you heard us say some things that suggested that kids can be a challenge and, frankly, a pain sometimes, but you missed the part where Mr. McHugh and I agreed that, no matter how challenging, stressful, expensive, and trying our kids might be, we wouldn't change places with anyone who has a quiet, organized life. You and the girls fill our family with life and energy. Watching Beth, Nate and now Gracie, Katie and you grow up is the greatest joy of our lives.

I'm sure Mr. McHugh feels the same about his kids. Also, he probably gets happiness from watching lots of kids in this town growing up. You had a negative reaction to just part of the story. Remember what happened with Leo the Lawnmower when you first came to live with us? We returned Leo, but we would never, let me repeat, NEVER wish that we could send you away. Get back **'on the same page,'** son, and get that project finished! I'll bet Mrs. Davenport and Mr. Arnold will think you did an <u>A</u>bsolutely <u>A</u>mazing, <u>A</u>wesome project. I'm very proud of you, Kevin."

I finished my project just in time to turn it in. I spent the last part of the report telling my class: "I enjoy being with Mr. McHugh. He is kind, thoughtful, funny, generous, and totally interested in the kids who come to his gym. Finally, I think he's the kind of person who deserves to have good things said about him for all the great things he does for our community."

I got an A- on my project. Mr. Arnold and Mrs. Davenport loved the pictures I sent in along with my report. but I forgot to make a cover for the whole thing. I guess, once again, I listened to only part of the instructions (the
report directions) and missed hearing that I needed a cover. Some things a guy never seems to learn!

# BREAK A LEG

## Gracie

**M**ost kids want to be involved in school activities like sports, arts and crafts, science experiments, and musical plays. That's *my* favorite thing. I love singing in front of people. It's a lot of work, but once we all get on the stage, the work becomes play.

This year, our class is working on the musical "Annie." I hoped to get the role of Annie, but my classmate Sue is a better singer than I am. So I was given the role of understudy if she can't perform when scheduled. It's a lot of work because I have to learn all the songs and speaking parts as if I were Annie. I also have a smaller part as one of the girls in the orphanage. That was fun because we have speaking parts as well as dancing, and we make fun of the woman who runs the orphanage. Now, it's just three days until showtime!

Today at supper, I reminded my mom and dad that the play was this week—Friday at 7 p.m."You have to come to our play on Friday. We've worked so hard. Kevin has worked on constructing the sets that Katie helped to design and decorate. I'm a girl at the orphanage, unless Sue gets sick or hurt, then I would get to be Annie. I guess I shouldn't want her to be unable to be Annie, but I would really like to sing 'The Sun Will Come Out Tomorrow.'"

"Gracie, you're struggling with something that happens to all of us. We envy the person who has something we would like to have, but we also know it would be wrong to wish bad luck on someone who has something we want. Give your best effort to the part you have. And, if Sue plays Annie, congratulate her later. That's being a good sport."

Friday morning I had to bug my mom one more time:

"Please say you'll get us to school at 6:30 p.m. We really want you to see how hard we've worked."

"We'll get you there on time tonight, honey—promise."

It was hard to concentrate on our schoolwork in the morning on Friday, but after lunch we had our last rehearsal. Everything went very well. When the school bell rang at 3 p.m. we had to go home and try not to think about our big performance tonight. We were too excited to eat, so Mom was very understanding and let us sit at the table and nibble at some food.

We got back to the school at 6:30 p.m. Everything was ready to go. My friends and I got dressed; then we spent too much time watching our families and friends file into the gym.

"I'm so nervous," said Sue. "Look at all those people. I don't think I can do this."

"Yes, you can," said Ms. Greene, our director. "You've practiced hard; you know your lines and the songs. You can do this, Sue, really, you can. Take a few deep breaths. Remember *The Little Engine That Could*, 'I think I can, I think I can.'" Now, all of you go out there and **'Break a Leg!'"**

At 7 p.m. the lights flickered, and we all took our places on the stage or in the wings. The curtain opened to lots of applause and cheering from the audience. We all looked at each other and took a deep breath. We were ready . . .

The performance was fantastic. Our school band played each song perfectly. Sue was awesome. She got lots of applause at the end. The whole cast bowed to the audience and then fell apart.

"Oh my gosh, that was so much fun."

"I was so scared—I thought I'd forget all my lines, but I didn't."

"Did you see your parents in the audience? I saw mine."

"I think there was a reporter from the Rainbow Falls newspaper. Maybe we'll be famous!"

We went into the cafeteria for a post-play party. It was

fun to listen to all the parents and teachers tell us how good we were. Our parents were the most expressive in telling us how much they enjoyed seeing us. I think many of the parents were surprised at how talented and brave their kids are. I was standing next to Fr. Mike, who comes to everything the kids in his parish do. I asked him, "What does **'Break a Leg'** mean, and why would you say that to someone who's about to go on stage?"

"It may have been a superstition from a long time ago, Gracie, like if you tell someone, 'Good Luck,' the opposite will happen, so if you say, **'Break a Leg'**, the performer will have good luck and have a good time. Looks like it worked well for all of you tonight."

On the way home, our parents had only good things to say about us: "Kevin, the sets were fantastic, Katie, the decorations were very realistic, and Gracie, you were very funny as a bratty little girl. I wanted to stand up and yell, 'Gracie, behave yourself!' It was a fun evening. You all should feel very proud of your hard work."

*Truth be told—we were!*

# THE BALL IS IN YOUR COURT

## Dad (Greg)

"We nead to get ready for Becky's Mother's Day and birthday celebrations. Mom's out of the house today until about 4 p.m. She's helping out Fr. Mike at the church." I looked around at the group assembled with me in our dining room: the kids' grandparents, Mitch and Maddie, uncles Bill and Tim, and the children, Gracie, Kevin, and Katie.

"Lucky for us, Mother's Day comes first. That's the easy one to plan. We'll go to church on Sunday morning; then I've made reservations at the Rainbow Falls Bed and Breakfast. The owners, Pat and Linda, serve the most delicious holiday brunch —ever! When I made the reservation, Linda told me she would give us a special deal for the occasion, given that we will have so many people there. In addition to all of us, Beth, Nate, and their families will join us, too. And we invited Fr. Mike to come if he isn't too busy. That's 11 adults, three children, and two toddlers."

"That's a really good idea, Greg. I've heard great reviews about that Mother's Day Brunch," Uncle Bill acknowledged. "I'm already looking forward to it."

"Me, too," chimed in Kevin, who was known for his love of food—all kinds and lots of it.

"Now, there's also the matter of a gift. It's really hard to shop for someone who always says she has more than she needs and doesn't want us to spend money on her. Any ideas rattling around in your heads?"

Unfortunately, there was an awfully long silence. I hoped it meant that everyone was thinking.

"I'll bet she would like an updated picture of our whole family to put on the cabinet in the dining room," Kevin offered as a suggestion.

"That's a great idea, Kevin," agreed Uncle Bill, "but you know what? How about if we made this her birthday gift? That would give us an extra day to get a group picture of all of us at the B and B brunch when our whole family will be there. That would make our project so much easier and less stressful. We have the equipment to prepare the picture. All we need to do is buy a new frame. Tim, you have expertise in the area of photography. Why don't you handle the picture-taking? You can count on me to find a suitable frame."

"Swell," I exclaimed. "Starting now, **'The Ball is in Your Court,'** OK?" (That means it's up to both of them to make the decisions and do the work to get the picture taken and framed.)

'It's also up to all of us to complete our tasks for Becky's Mother's Day celebration. What will we do for a Mother's Day gift?"

"Gee, Dad, you always say that we need to find a gift that's personal, not like a kitchen utensil or appliance. It's hard to think of something for Mom. She has us, what more does she need?" asked Kevin.

*"A week's vacation at a spa,"* I thought.

Gracie and Katie had been very quiet throughout this whole discussion. Just as I decided they were in another world right now, Katie announced, "I know what we can get Mom! You know how she wears that ratty old sweater around the house when she feels cold? What if we got her a new sweater, one that she could wear inside or outside of the house—a super nice one?"

"That's a wonderful idea, Katie. What do you think about that suggestion, Gracie?" (I had to ask because sometimes the girls would disagree with each other just for the fun of being irritating.)

"I like that idea. In fact, I was in Rhonda's Boutique with Mom last week and she saw a sweater she liked. She held it up to herself and asked me what I thought of it. I told her it looked very pretty. I think she would be happy with that sweater as her gift."

"You know, Dad, Mom likes to be warm and comfy around the house. Maybe Gracie and I could go to the Thrift Store tomorrow and find a soft, used sweater or flannel shirt that she could wear around the house when she's working. She wouldn't want to wear the new one to do housework."

"Another very sensible suggestion." I looked around at the group—all the heads were nodding in agreement.

"I'd love to drive Katie and Gracie wherever they need to go tomorrow," volunteered Mitch. " I've got nothing else to do."

"That's really helpful, Grandpa. We need to go to two different places, and then come home and wrap our gifts. Yes, I know Dad, **'the ball is in our court,'**" said Katie.

"Perhaps we need to have a calm meal tonight instead of our usually outrageous Fabulous Friday dinner and put our energy toward a Marvelous Monday treat?" I asked and saw lots of heads nod.

"That's a good idea," agreed Kevin. "I'll be glad to work on tonight's dinner. How about pizza or mac and cheese?" (Kevin seldom offered to help with cooking a meal, so we decided to take advantage of his generosity.) "Who wants to work with me?" Kevin asked, clearly afraid he might be working all alone.

"I'll help you, honey," offered Maddie. "It will give me a good opportunity to get to know you better. Besides, I make some wicked brownies."

"I'll help, too." Gracie wanted to be included in what she hoped might be fun. "I'll set the table."

"OK," I responded, "that sounds like a great plan."

"Yes," exclaimed the Unfabulous Friday meal team.

"How will we get Becky out of the house on Monday so we can get everything ready?" Maddie had a worried look on her face.

"Thelma Ann, our librarian, will contact Becky Sunday and tell her she's needed to work in the afternoon on Monday because one of the volunteers is ill and has to stay home. Becky always says 'yes' to those kinds of requests. She'll be gone from 1-

4:00 p.m."

"Who wants to be in charge of her birthday dinner? It probably shouldn't include mac and cheese or pizza," I said, jokingly. When Maddie looked interested, but not wanting to be in charge of everything, I jumped in to offer my help. "I know what her favorite meal is—linguine with a bunch of chopped veggies in a butter sauce. It's easy to make and delicious to eat."

"I chopped the veggies last time," Kevin reminded him.

"Yes, kiddo, I remember, especially when you cut your finger chopping the onions."

"It was a small cut, Dad; besides, I like working with knives."

"As a detective, son, that statement scares me somewhat." But I smiled and said we would welcome his help.

"What about you, Bill? You've been awfully quiet so far. How can we put you to work?" I like to tease my brother.

"I thought I might get the birthday cake on Monday. I'm a real connoisseur when it comes to desserts—almost as talented as Kevin. He and I could put our heads together after this meeting and come up with a delicious cake. Yes, the **'ball is in our court'** for this. We'll run with it. You can count on us."

Kevin offered to order several pizzas with different toppings; Mattie got ready to make the brownies. That left me to wander through the kitchen and pantry looking for ingredients for Becky's birthday dinner. With a little bit of luck, we wouldn't have to do much grocery shopping.

That night, dinner was more subdued. We hadn't been together for a while, all of us, so we spent our time in that unusual pastime—conversation—visiting and catching up on what each of us had been doing. School was coming to an end in a few weeks, so Tim, Maddie and Mitch wanted to know if we had summer plans. And we teased our grandparents about their busy lifestyle, now that both of them are retired. Seems like they are always moving: by planes, trains, automobiles, and cruise ships. Before we left the table, we thanked Kevin for his delicious choices of pizza and Maddie for her yummy brownies.

Right after dinner, having divided up all the chores, Kevin and Bill put their cake-loving heads together. Gracie, Katie and Mitch agreed on a time to go shopping tomorrow. Tim and I offered to clean up the kitchen, and then sat at the dining room table with the other adults drinking coffee and enjoying a quiet time to talk with each other. After a little while, Maddie and Mitch left for their hotel room and Kevin got comfy on the couch in the living room so his uncle Tim could sleep in his bed upstairs. By 9 o'clock, everyone was in bed. Becky asked me what I had done all afternoon. I told her, "I had an extremely important meeting with some very high-level, capable people."

On Saturday, everyone executed their assignments as planned. Bill ordered the birthday cake, Mitch and the girls went shopping, Maddie and I talked about coordinating the birthday meal. We enlisted Kevin to call Mrs. Hannon's Toy Store to order a dozen balloons that would be inflated and ready on Monday afternoon. He and his grandpa would get them.

That night, Tim, Bill, Maddie and Mitch went out for dinner. The five of us ate as our regular-sized family and played Monopoly afterwards. Becky was the big property owner. The rest of us will be in her debt forever . . .

On Sunday, we awoke to a day that promised to be beautiful. It had rained during the night, so the air was fresh. Now the sky was blue with only a few wispy clouds remaining. We couldn't have asked for a nicer day. We met up with Bill and the Lanoskis at the church. Fr. Mike did a wonderful job of welcoming all the women, asking God's blessing on all the mothers and on all women who nurture others in some way. It was a cheerful and heart-warming celebration.

After the service, we walked slowly toward the Bed and Breakfast. It sits near the river, so we watched the water rush over the rocks. Snowmelt in the mountains provided us with clear, cold water. We met Beth and Nate with their spouses Ed and Julie, and children, Griffin and Haley, who were just learning to walk. The restaurant was decorated so beautifully.

"Welcome, how great to see all of you. Glad you could join us today. We have a large table set for all of you, and two highchairs for the little ones. Please, follow me." Pat was the epitome of hospitality. Linda was waiting for us at the table. After we were seated and had ordered drinks, she explained how to choose our meal from the many choices at the buffet. Needless to say, Kevin was in 7$^{th}$ Heaven.

After eating, but before going to the buffet for dessert, we toasted Becky, Maddie, Beth and Julie and wished them a Happy Mother's Day. The girls brought out the two wrapped gifts. One at a time Becky opened them and told all of us that the first sweater was the beautiful one she had seen at the Boutique, and the flannel shirt was so soft, she was sure it would keep her warm whenever she felt cold in the house. She thanked all of us and hugged Gracie and Katie. Nate gave his wife, Julie, a ring with a green stone for Haley's birthday. Beth's husband, Ed, gave her a sun hat. After that, we toasted the women again. Then, Tim went out into the B and B back yard facing the river and set up a tripod so we could take our pictures in a beautiful setting. Because we wanted all our family members in it, we used the timer on the camera. Luckily, digital cameras let you see the picture immediately to determine if it's suitable or not. It took us a few tries, but we got a great picture of the whole group. We decided to take some other group pictures tomorrow, since we would all be together again.

When the little ones began to cry, and our kids got restless, we decided to head for home so everyone could change their clothes and get comfortable. The rest of the day was open for whatever people wanted to do. We all agreed to gather at our house the next day for Becky's birthday, starting at 2 p.m., for the execution of all of our assigned tasks.

When Becky left for the library and school was over,

Kevin and Bill went to get the cake. After that, Kevin and Mitch drove to the toy store to pick up the balloons. Tim had already worked on getting the perfect family picture ready and placed in the frame Greg and Gracie had purchased on Saturday.

Gracie set the table with the extra place settings belonging to Nate, Julie, Beth, Ed, Tim, Bill and, hope fully, Fr. Mike. The toddlers would have high chairs near their parents. Kevin and Mitch brought home the balloons, which were immediately taped to various places in the dining room. They put a balloon on each high chair to give the little ones something to look at as their parents tapped the balloons back and forth.

Maddie and I didn't have to make dinner until Becky got home because it was pretty simple and needed to be hot when we ate it. Kevin could cut up some veggies while I cooked the linguine, and Maddie got the big pot ready with some melted butter to receive all the pasta and veggies. At the last minute, all the ingredients would be stirred together in the big pot.

When Becky walked into the house, she was astonished at all the work that had been done to make the dining room look so festive. We were all cleaned up, and it just took a while for her to run upstairs and change her clothes. When she came downstairs, she exclaimed, "Wow! How did you manage all this without me knowing anything?" We believe that she was truly surprised that we had done so much to prepare for her birthday.

While she sat in the living room and talked to her son and daughter and their spouses, she seemed to take particular delight in watching her grandchildren, Haley and Griffin, make valiant attempts to cross the room from one parent to another on their wobbly legs.

Several people went into the backyard and played croquet until they were called to come in, wash their hands, and sit down at the table. With 11 adults and three children at the table, we had added an extra card table and chairs to the end of our fairly large dining room table. Even though we were a little squished, no one seemed to mind. Kevin had cut (successfully) all the tomatoes, onions, black olives and artichoke hearts before his mom got home. I cooked the linguine when Becky came home, and Maddie prepared the big serving pot.

At 5:30 p.m. we were ready to eat. It didn't take us long to fill our plates, reach for a dinner roll and butter, and wait for someone to pray. That someone was my brother, Bill, whom I know has loved Becky for as long as I have. In his eyes, she is a wonderful wife, mother, and sister-in-law. In his prayer he asked God to bless and protect her, and then asked God to bless all of us and the meal we were about to share. It made all of us smile and look at Becky, who had tears in her eyes.

As usual at every birthday or holiday, we pray, then a certain amount of time is dedicated to eating and praising the cooks. But then, without fail, the jokes begin:

> Katie: "What did the ewe receive as a gift for Mother's day? A: A spaaaaaa day ." ***

> Kevin: "Why don't they have Mother's Day sales? A: Because Moms are priceless!" ***

> Gracie: "What do dogs wear on their heads when it's cold outside? A: Ear Mutts" ***

> Bill: Why would frog wait for a bus?
> A: Because his car got toad." ***

> Tim: "How did the candy rescue the person lost at sea? A: It was a Life Saver." ***

> Beth: "Where do snowmen get their daily weather report? A: From the winternet " ***

> Becky: "Why did the teacher jump into the ocean? A: To test the waters" ***

> Mitch: "What do you call a thieving alligator? A: A Crookodile" ***

> Fr. Mike: "What kind of bird is always on pitch in the choir? A: A Hummingbird" ***

187

Nate: "What happened to a shark who swallowed a bunch of keys?
A: He got lockjaw." ***

Me: "What do you call a car that's always thirsty? A : A gas guzzler" ***

Nate's wife Julie: "What's a watch's eldest relative? A : Grandfather clock ***

Beth's husband Ed: "Where do dogs go to make new friends? A: Fire hydrants" ***

Maddie: "How do you send a letter to the Easter Bunny  A: By hare mail' ***

When the groans and giggles subsided, Bill and I went to the kitchen to bring out the cake. We had lit candles in the shape of a 47. We sang *Happy Birthday* and after she blew out the candles, we clapped and took the cake back into the kitchen to cut it.

Meanwhile, Maddie, Tim and the three kids cleared the tables and put a stack of dessert plates next to the cake. One by one, a plate of cake was delivered to each person. Becky got hers first, but she was willing to wait until all of us were ready to dig in to the yummy looking cake.

Before the dessert plates were removed, Bill and Tim handed Becky her birthday gift. She opened it very gently, saving the paper for another time. When she saw the picture from the day before now placed in a new frame, she gave a gasp: "This is beautiful. And to think you did this just yesterday!"

"When we want to, we can move very quickly," Tim informed her. Bill placed the picture on the accent cabinet against the wall in the dining room. Many of our family pictures are there.

"By the way, honey, I think you look lovely in your new sweater," Greg said, admiring his wife. "Good choice, Katie and

Gracie." The girls beamed as they looked at their mom.

Nate and Beth gave her a certificate to a nail salon in town. Just the thought of having her nails done made her smile.

"Hey," interrupted Bill, "we were going to take pictures of each family group. Why don't we get pictures of Nate and Beth's family before the little ones fall asleep? It'll only take a minute." We divided the group up into family pictures that would include Tim, Bill, Mitch, Maddie, Julie and Ed. Each group moved quickly into place to sit on our stairway going up to the bedrooms. We changed from group to group as we all wanted to be in several pictures with the people we love. It was a great way to end the evening.

By the time Fr. Mike, the Lanoskis, Beth and Nate's families, and Bill left, we had the kitchen and dining room clean. It was definitely a group effort. I was so impressed that everyone in the room tonight **'took the ball when it was in their court'** and worked to give Becky the birthday she deserved.

***funnyeditor.com.

# I'VE GOT YOUR BACK

## The Stewart Family

School is out; life has slowed down. There are lots of things for our kids to do, but as the days go on, they seem to be getting a little bored. However, when they realized that both Father's Day and our annual ritual called *Gotcha Day*—the day the three kids were adopted—are coming up in a week, the middle of June now seems to be a very exciting time. Our whole family, uncles Tim and Bill, our five kids (three twelve-year olds, two older adult kids) and their spouses, (Ed and Julie, and toddlers, Haley and Griffin) are coming. We realized that this was going to be a joyous time for all of us. Our special friends Maddie and Mitch have other plans back at their home, but our very good friend Fr. Mike hopes to come.

Father's Day is such a special day to tell the men in our lives how much we appreciate them. My husband, Greg, along with Bill, Tim, Nate, Ed, and even Fr. Mike deserve special recognition for the way they nurture all of us. So we've planned a fun-filled day with great food served in our backyard. Nate has offered to be the BBQ chef, while everyone else brings a pot luck dish. Gracie, Kevin, and Katie have to come up with their own contributions, which usually include marshmallows, sticks, chocolate squares and ice cream. This is in addition to the cakes we get for Father's Day and *Gotcha Day*.

<u>Beth:</u>
As a family, we all get into *Gotcha Day*, the day Gracie, Katie and Kevin were adopted into the Stewart clan. Nate and I were 24 and 23 years old when Mom and Dad told us we were going to have a brother and two sisters, age nine. That was quite a shock. At first we thought they were crazy to want

to go through all the work of raising of a new crop of kids, but honestly, they're doing a terrific job with the munchkins, without leaving Nate and I feeling ignored or like the nine-year-olds are their new and improved family. It's Mom and Dad's job to find suitable gifts for the three kids to celebrate this anniversary.

Bill:

As Greg's brother, I was so happy to find that the three kids had been transferred to Rainbow Falls and put into Becky and Greg's care until they were eligible for adoption. Being their new Uncle Bill is a real treat for me. Then, less then a year ago, Tim, the long-lost brother of the kids' moms discovered that he had two nieces and a nephew. Thankfully, he couldn't wait to meet them. Now Uncle Tim is a welcome addition to our family. The two of us are in charge of finding a gift for Greg for Father's Day.

Tim:

This Sunday is a super, double-duty party. The Stewarts love to party, so even though I'm the newest Uncle to the team, and this is my first *Gotcha Day*, I know things will go well—*minor goofs to be expected!*

We teased Fr. Mike that he had the most important task—to pray for a beautiful day. So far, the weather forecast was for lots of sun and warm temperatures.

On Sunday, a beautiful June day, the three kids, Greg, Bill, Tim and I went to church, where Fr. Mike welcomed all dads and all men who find ways to nurture kids or anyone who needs some help. It was a very thoughtful and joyous celebration. Even Fr. Mike heard a number of *"Happy Father's Day"* greetings. Greg and I, with the three kids, decided to skip the coffee hour after church in order to go home, change into more comfortable clothes and have an early, simple lunch. Bill, Tim and Fr. Mike sat in the church hall for a while enjoying a fresh cup of coffee and each other's company.

At about 3 p.m. the rest of our family started to arrive. Tim and Bill came a little before Ed, so they got the lawn chairs out of the garage and the high chairs from the basement. When Ed arrived, they moved the picnic table to the center of the yard and added chairs at the ends of the table. Our table is long enough to hold four people per side, so we had to put two lawn chairs and a high chair at each end of the table. It was a little crowded, but it was fun to rub elbows with the people we love.

Of course, no Stewart family gathering could happen without a few jokes. Halfway through the meal, they began:

Greg: "Hey, Fr. Mike, if you need help building an ark...A: I Noah guy." ***

Gracie: "Where did the school kittens go for their field trip? A: A Mew-zeum" ***

Bill: "What do you call a pencil with two erasers A: Pointless" ***

Katie "What did the cat say when it fell off the dining room table?
A: Me-owch ***

Mom: "Why couldn't the couple get married at the library?
A: It was booked." ***

Beth: "Where do baby ghosts go during the day? A: Dayscare" ***

Fr. Mike: "What book do people use who can't sing in church? A: A humnal" ***

Tim: "Why does Rudolf love to get wet? A: Because he's a reindeer." ***

Julie: "Why did the baby cookie cry?
A: Because his mother was a wafer
   so long."

Nate: "Why did Mickey Mouse become
an astronaut?
A: Because he wanted to visit Pluto." ***

Kevin: "What's an astronaut's favorite
sandwich? A: Launch meat." ***

Ed: "Why do plants hate algebra?
A: It gives them square roots." ***

By this time, everyone was finished eating, so we cleared off the plates and silverware, and got ready to prepare the dessert. Nate had made sure the fire in our small outdoor pit would continue to burn for a while so that the kids could have their fill of S'mores. The cake for the fathers in attendance and one for our *Gotcha Kids*, Katie, Kevin, and Gracie Stewart were brought out, along with ice cream to accompany each cake. All of us had lots to choose from. Now, there was very little conversation because all of us were busy eating.

Finally, we cleaned up once more and returned to our seats. The kids stood by the fire for a short time, making their last dessert for the evening. When they sat down, we brought out the gifts for all the people whose lives we were celebrating.

Since his birthday, my husband, Greg, has gone golfing a few times when the course had no snow. He liked it well enough to want to move beyond the three clubs he had and invest in a few more. Bill and Tim got him a golf bag for all the items he needed to carry around the course. I bought two clubs for him that he had been talking about, and the twins and Gracie got him a fashionable hat to wear that was made with the Stewart clan's tartan, plus matching covers for his clubs. Fr. Mike gave him a St. Christopher medal (saint for the protection of travelers) to keep him safe as he walked (wandered) those 18 holes.

Uncle Bill got a new pair of golf gloves from Greg and me, and some balls and tees from the kids. Beth and Nate paid his greens dues for 4 months.

Uncle Tim figured he was too new to the family, so he wasn't expecting a gift, but our family got him a new hard-shelled carry-on suitcase, hoping that he would continue to come visit us.

Several of us went together to get Nate and Ed tickets to the antique auto show coming to Riverview in early July.

And Fr. Mike got a gift certificate from the kids to the Toy Store where he can get comic books for his younger niece and nephew or for himself whenever he needs a break from work. (I *think our family members are the only ones who know of his secret love.*)

When all the men were finished expressing their gratitude, Beth and Becky handed the three munchkins identical packages. When they opened them, Kevin had a metal dish, Katie had a pack of tennis balls, and Gracie had a leash. It took a minute for their brains to put together the gifts and the one thing that was missing. Suddenly, Nick, the director of the animal shelter, appeared from the side of the house with a 6–month-old black dog. When Gracie saw him, she shouted, "It's Max, from the shelter. He's a rescue dog!" She jumped up and raced to him. Since she's been volunteering at the shelter for a while, she sees dogs come in each week. She's been talking about Max for two weeks. Clearly, the dog recognized her voice and became very excited. Kevin and Katie raced over and fell to their knees, hugging the dog. The look on their faces was sheer joy.

"Can we keep him, Dad? Is he really ours?" Gracie asked, almost afraid this was just a visit.

"Yes, kids, Max is ours. It's his *Gotcha Day,* too. But it will be YOUR job to take care of him. We'll talk about your responsibilities tomorrow. Kevin, please fill the water dish for him."

After all the excitement faded, and Max seemed to settle down and lie behind the kids, Nick said, "Nice to meet all of you," and left. Greg stood up and gave a little cough to get our attention. "I think I can speak for everyone today who either gave or received a gift. This family is truly blessed by generosity and thankfulness. Yet there's another characteristic of our family. **'We Have Each Other's Back.'"**

"What does that mean, Dad?" When Gracie asked, the twins looked at me.

"In my line of work, I'm sometimes in some dangerous situations. That's why police officers seldom work alone. We always have another officer with us to **'have our back.'** People who **'have each other's back'** are prepared to support them, protect them, and do what's best for them. This past year I've seen this kind of behavior among all of our family members. It makes me very happy and proud of each one of you."

Then, in an unspoken gesture, each member of our family reached out and touched the back of a person or persons next to them. Each of the kids stretched out one hand to touch Max. *My guess is that soon this dog will **'have our backs,'** too.*

***funnyeditor.com

# ACKNOWLEDGMENTS

I would like to thank the following people who were invaluable to me in the creation of this book:

---Barb T. and Hank (at UPS) for their help with the cover design

---Proofreaders: Barb N., Sherry A., and Karen H. They found more mistakes than I ever thought were possible! (And there may be more!)

---I also need to recognize and thank the people at

funnyeditor.com.
Reactive Resources, LLC 1344 Disk Drive #1060
Sparks, NV89436

who graciously allowed me to use many of their jokes. ( Some of them are really groaners!)

Kathy
May 2023

Made in the USA
Coppell, TX
04 October 2023

22418453R00108